Glacier

A Boy. An Island. A Prophecy.

Peter Shearing

Published: 2022 by Leschenault Press
Leschenault, Western Australia

ISBN: 9781922670687 - Paperback Edition
ISBN: 9781922670755 - E-Book Edition
*** *** *

Cover Design by Brittany Wilson | Brittwilsonart.com

To my wife,

Anne

Prologue
(present day)

It's cold!

So cold.

So dark.

So lonely!

How long have I been here?

Hours?

Days?

Years?

I have waited so long for Bu'sa- the Earth Goddess- to wrap me in her bosom and carry me to her home to join my ancestors. I have failed her, and my spirit will wander the infernos of Xi'tan for all time.

I wait.

I see a radiant light.

It slowly brightens.

The darkness slowly ebbs and a glowing brilliance takes its place.

I wait.

Soon I hear voices. They sound like the grumbling of Ra'barak, the Thunder God, in the distance.

The voices become louder.

Two shadowy figures clad in strange coloured skins loom over me.

Are they Bu'sa's envoys?

They disappear, leaving me alone again.

Soon I hear more voices, more excited this time. Figures appear over me once more.

I hear banging in the distance; the ground shakes and my body is moved.

I feel arms moving below me, lifting me and placing me in what seems to be a sarcophagus.

I hear scraping and the light disappears as a lid covers me.

As I am closed back into darkness once again, I hear a word uttered by one of the figures: "Otzi!"

Pursuit
(3000 BCE)

We trotted through a grove of fir trees, the sound of our feet softened by the carpet of needles on the ground. We paused, listening for our pursuers. Our breath came in puffs of mist in the crisp alpine air. Chabish and I crouched low among the underbrush as in the distance we heard the crack of a foot on a twig.

They were close, very close.

My heart was pounding as I recalled the last few weeks, still vivid in my memory.

There had been a stirring in the village as rumours from our hunting parties had spread that there were gangs of armed warriors roaming the distant hills, burning and looting whatever they found. The villagers had noted that there were distant clouds of smoke beyond the hills, but this was attributed to burning in preparation of ploughing and laying fallow of new pasture.

Then a rag-tag and motley collection of what appeared to be beggars made their unwanted appearance. As soon as we heard them speak in our tongue, we realised our mistake and that they were of our kin. One of the group, a tall and, in a way handsome, blonde man insisted on speaking with our clan's chief, Bontag. After conversing privately in his hut for several hours, Bontag and the stranger re-emerged. Bontag looked very haggard and drawn as he walked to the centre of the village. He then gathered all the clan's elders and the High priest, Isatru, to meet in the High priest's hut. Chabish, being an elder, followed them in.

When Chabish and the others came out, they too looked very concerned.

"What is happening?" I asked.

"There are raiders in the hills from the lands on the other side of the mountains. We have not seen them before, and they are not of our people. Bontag has told us to use all caution if out hunting. We will also need to place sentries around our village," he answered despondently, and then added, "if they come, our womenfolk and children are not safe. These people here are from a village only three days walk away, and they are all that is left of 100 villagers. Their menfolk had their throats cut and heads severed, their womenfolk defiled, murdered and their children taken into slavery. The paths in their village flowed with blood, it was only through the Gods' grace that they escaped alive."

A few of the other menfolk listened sombrely to Chabish. Then one rallied, "let us gather our warriors and go flush these piles of sheep's dung, these pestilences from a whore's bed, and drive them back over the mountains!"

A murmur of approval ran through them.

"No!" a voice boomed over the rising din, and Bontag strode amongst them. "There will be no war party! What do you hope to achieve if our menfolk are slaughtered and our womenfolk are left to defend themselves? Nothing!" he stated firmly, "Nothing! We are farmers. Farmers! Our warriors have not fought in an age and I fear that they have gotten fat and lazy.

Yes, we will defend ourselves if attacked, but we will not run after them."

Then Bontag's voice softened as he spoke directly to the younger menfolk. "All of you, gather your weapons and make them keen and sharp. Have them ready at your side, there will be a constant guard at all times. You are to heed the advice and demands of the elders at all times. To disregard them, death will be your reward."

Bontag turned abruptly on his heel and went back into his hut.

A murmur of foreboding spread throughout the village. Womenfolk gathered the children and hustled them inside the huts while menfolk gathered in small groups discussing these events. A group of young men, recently admitted to manhood, stirred near Bontag's hut, a rumble of discontent apparent among them. In their bravado, they noisily announced their intention of disobeying Bontag and to go and fight. However, this showy display of embryonic bravery was short-lived as Bontag re-appeared at the doorway of his hut, glowering sullenly at the group. One by one they looked at him and then sulked away, all vestiges of valour and gallantry had vanished. Village life returned to a semblance of normality.

Over the following days the villagers continued tending their crops and animals. This, the cultivation of crops and the domestication of sheep and native goats, had been an established custom for over a thousand summers now as each generation handed down its legacy to the next. The weather in the foothills of the giant mountains, which rose with their snow-capped heads into the not-too-distant horizon, was extremely generous for this lifestyle. Wheat and maize could easily be grown with harvests rich and surpluses plentiful. Flax was grown to be woven into coarse cloth and the sheep and goats provided wool to be spun into clothing, as well as a staple of meat for the appetites of the clan.

Chabish and I retreated to what we did best, tending the furnace where blocks of copper- a reddish coloured metal- were melted to cast tools for the crops and now, weapons to protect our very livelihoods. When not tending this, we would chase game and birds to feed Chabish's family.

Some days later, Chabish and I were out hunting on the lower hills above the village. We were both armed with bows and knives, and Chabish also carried a short spear hooked with his quiver on his back. Sem'a, the Sun God, was starting her long rest and the days were colder where her breath now chilled the air. Our hunt up to that time was unfruitful as we had seen no game at all. We had only observed some geese in the heavens, but they were too far away to get with either spear or arrow.

Suddenly we heard a scream, it echoed up from a thicket of trees in a shallow valley. As we crept closer we saw three men, they were not of Chabish's village, and were dressed as the savages from the distant north. Two had a young woman held down by her hair and arms while the third held a knife against her slender neck. She screamed again as she kicked at her attackers frantically. I looked at Chabish and he already had an arrow poised on his bow with the string drawn back. Swish! The arrow took flight and found its mark – the neck of the third savage. With a look of surprise on his face, blood began streaming from the wound in his neck and very quickly he crumpled to the ground, shaking and jerking for a moment before stopping still. The other two savages let go of the woman and reached around to pick up their spears.

Swish! Another arrow found its target and the second savage fell backwards, the arrow protruding from his eye socket. I felt ill as I strung an arrow to my bow – I detested the thought of killing a fellow man, but the gods would forgive me in this instance. The third turned and ran as my own arrow found its mark between his shoulders. He fell to his knees then tried to get up and run again. Quickly we each plucked arrows from our backs and let them loose. Both arrows hit almost simultaneously, one through his neck, the other through the right side of his chest. With a loud gurgle he fell on his face and choked in his own blood.

We ran through the trees to the thicket but found that the woman had fled, maybe she feared that we would do the same as the savages. But now we feared that there may be more of them close by as they were probably in a war party. Our fears were well founded as we soon heard the crashing through the undergrowth of the remainder of the barbarians. We sprinted back up the hill keeping low and hidden by the trees. When we reached the top, we found a rocky outcrop from where we could clearly see our adversary and how many there were. A breath caught in my throat as I counted about 20 of them, covered in thick fur skins from head to knee, most with flint tipped spears and others with long bows and quivers full of arrows. Their faces were painted with streaks of blue and black, their hair tied back with eagle feathers adorning the back of their heads. They looked fearsome and they were out for blood – ours!

Suddenly one shouted. We had been spotted, so we hastily retreated further up the mountain. We felt that the higher we went, the less likely they would follow. We ran until we came to the first pillows of snow in the clefts and hollows. This was our territory, one which we were well accustomed to. Unfortunately, we failed to realize that this was one which they were also very familiar with, having come from the mountains to the north. As we ran, darkness slowly enveloped us and in the fading twilight we heard our pursuers fall further behind until their voices were lost in the silence of the mountain.

Before all light left us, we found what appeared to be a natural fort of rocks deposited by a long-ago deluge forming a wall around a rocky knoll. Here we rested, vigilant and unable to sleep had we wanted to, listening very carefully for any sound coming from the valley below. Apart from some snorting from an alpine animal and the occasional creak of a tree, there was nothing. I carefully shifted across so that I could see more of the valley over a low rock in the wall. Far below, I could see the flickering light of flames and the constant movement of people about it. By my reckoning they would have been about two to three hours away, since they had a steep climb from their campsite to ours.

Abruptly, the fire sparked high with flames shooting skywards. A shout was heard and I could see several figures running madly around, their garments alight. Then I heard the screams, like a tortured ghoul caught up in the flames of the underworld. I called softly to Chabish, who had also heard the cries, and came to my side to see. Again, there was a shout and in the dying flames I could vaguely make out figures falling. Then it was quiet again, only broken by a far-off moan and cry.

What had happened? We would have to wait till daylight to find out.

In the stillness of the night, I thought of my home, so far away in time and distance. I could see and smell in my mind the fresh sweetness of the barley and wheat which my family grew. I wondered if Father and Mother were still alive, if Ka'deen's children also played among the steps of the great temple only to be chastised by the priests. I tried to imagine what the new temple would look like and indeed if it had even been completed yet. I could see Nee'sa, flouncing her loveliness along the path between the fields, her long blonde hair streaming behind her in the breeze, the trace of her femininity hazily apparent through the veil of her clothing. I thought of the mighty temple of Haja-rim overlooking the ocean, and the abode of the sea god, Ba'hah, on the little island of Fiffl. I thought of the subterranean beauty of Saffl'na where our ancestors had carved a temple from the rock for the souls of our departed, where we could leave those souls for Bu'sa to take with her to her home. I could only hold back the tears as these memories flooded my mind.

Island

I was given the name Ka'desh by my father at my birth. When I was very little I was told that it was the ancient word for "Anointed One" because, at the moment my eyes opened into the world, Sem'a the sun god sent a ray of her breath onto my brow. My family lived on a tiny scrap of land surrounded by the ocean, which we called Melita. It means "the land of honey", and was reflective of the colour of the soft stone found there. Our village had no particular name – it was just called Shema's place, or Ta'Shema, and was the name given to our community long ago. Like all villages on our island, it was but a cluster of round huts with walls built from rammed earth and clay and with woven grass roofs. The huts were communal dwellings for each family unit and could have up to 50 kinfolk living in each. Ours had been passed down from generation to generation and was given to my father as it was expected that the eldest son of each household would become head of the household on the passing of their papa. Always nearby to each village was a temple where we could gather to pray and make offerings to the gods. Unlike the communal houses where family lore related their history, the temples brooded over us – their builders names lost in time – forever watching and protecting. They stood grand and majestic as a silent witness to our ancestors and their lives. The priests and temple elders lived in an enclosure near the temple but set apart from the villagers so that they could retain their privacy in temple administrations. These people of the temples were revered greatly by all the villagers on the island for their wisdom and guidance.

Our land at times was a harsh land. The weather ranged from warm to very hot during the time of Sem'as breath, she being the god of warmth and bright light and living in her great ball of fire in the sky. There could be torrential rain and strong winds during the cooler times when Xita'klil, the god of rain and Ra'barak, the god of thunder, would roar and rumble their anger at each other as they tried to tear the earth asunder and lash it with torrents of water.

The islands were once covered with a thick forestation of fir and pine trees, but over the time these were denuded until only small pockets existed. As such the soil, once rich, fertile and heavily covering the underlying rock foundations, was now thin and a thing much treasured, with much of the soil having been blown or washed to sea.

Water was also a treasured commodity on our islands. We had no streams which flowed all year round. What creeks we had were wholly dependent upon Xita'klil sending forth his tears to flow for that moment. Our ancestors, with much foresight, had dug gigantic cisterns in the rock to store the water of Xita'klil's tears to quench the thirst of our crops during the drier time of the year. It also gave each village a readily available source for domestic use.

There was another island nearby called Ga'Desh, from where people came to trade with our villages. These people were close kinfolk but they spoke a coarser dialect of our language. They told us that they had a great temple which they called Jiaganta-meaning 'made by giants,', which they say was built by giant gods long, long ago. My father once promised us that he would one day lead us on a pilgrimage to see it. We needed, he said, to make our offerings to the sea god Ba'hah, to appease her and allow our safe passage as we crossed the water to get there. There were many, he told us earnestly, that did not do this and suffered the consequences of Ba'hah's rage as she churned the waters separating our two lands like an angry cauldron.

On occasions there were travellers from distant places who visited the villages close to the sea and traded with them. These people were not of our kin but came from strange and distant lands. Some spoke a language similar to our own but with enough words different to ours that understanding was sometimes difficult. They brought with them beautiful clay pottery, as well as a hard rock they called obsidian which was fashioned into jewellery and knife blades, and red ochre, a powder used in our funeral rites and as a decoration on our own earthenware.

My early childhood days were spent as any other child in our village. My older brother Ka'deen at 12 years, my seven cousins all younger than I, and myself at ten years, worked at our chores in the fields cultivating the coarse gravelly soil, careful not to dig too deep through the thin covering and blunting or breaking our bone tools. When not doing chores, we played among the rock walls enclosing our family's field, as well as around the massive walls of our temple. Several times, when we became too boisterous and noisy, the elders would come out and tell us very sternly to move on and play elsewhere quietly.

Although it seemed that I was accepted by my peers, I did most times prefer my own company. Ka'deen, being the elder of us two brothers, would often accompany his own friends who were much the same age as he, leaving me to my own devices. When playing with the other children who were my age, I would tend to follow rather than lead, which would on occasions lead to mischief and misadventure. Being the offspring of rather stern parents, we would quickly take ownership of any misadventure and face the repercussions accordingly, not taking any chances of being caught in a lie or worse.

As a child I was as inquisitive as any other about the wonders of the world surrounding us. Of an evening, my brother and I would sit at my father's feet and listen intently to stories of his own childhood and of the relationship the ancient's deep spirituality had to our land. Often, I would ask him about the temples and the gods we worshipped, which he would explain as best he could.

He related that, at the beginning of time, Sem'a the sun god of the day and Kamah the moon god of night, shone their light onto a desolate world. Our island did not exist at that time, and only the fires from Xi'tan's furnaces would flash through the barren earth to spill its molten contents down into the deep valleys. Sem'a was saddened by this and a tear from her only eye fell upon the dry earth. From that first tear, Xita'klil- the rain god- was born. He rose up into the sky to greet Sem'a and saw her great sadness. She explained that she wanted her land to be fertile and for other creatures to be created. Her sadness affected Xita'klil so much that torrents of his own tears fell upon the land so ravaged by the underworld fires. Xi'tan responded by spewing forth his fires to dry up Xita'klil's tears, but the tears turned to clouds and in turn fell as rain. Eventually Xita'klil prevailed, as his tears filled the deep valleys and plains and the first lands emerging above the churning waters. Sem'a and Xi'tan reconciled their differences and became lovers, eventually bearing a daughter, Ba'hah- the goddess of the sea- to calm the waters.

Xi'tan, jealous now of the harmony between the other gods, suddenly and savagely attacked Ba'hah. She fought him bravely but eventually his strength overwhelmed her. In their throes, a great land was pushed up to the north of their island and the sea surrounding them became bigger. Ba'hah, in deep shame, withdrew, closing the sea off to the rest of the world with the exception of a small channel far to the west. Impregnated with Xi'tan's seed, she eventually bore a son who she named Frott'i, whom she commanded to bring fruit and grain to the lands so that the brown earth may bear and sustain life.

Xita'klil saw Ba'hah's deep melancholy and to lift her spirits, called forth his cousin Ra'barak, the god of thunder, and charged him to send his bolts of lightning to the earth to charge the fledgling life there. At once trees, grasses and other plant life sprang from the ground. Animals grew from the rocks and stones and populated the island. Ba'hah tore open her chest and threw one of her ribs to the earth from which man and woman grew.

From these very early beginnings our people prospered, populating the lands. Soon, several clans looked over the waters and saw clouds forming at the far edge of the sea. In time they constructed rafts of timber and, loading the rafts with food, animals, tools and seed for planting, started the dangerous passage towards the clouds. For a few days the sea was flat with only a wisp of dry, gentle wind which they called the grigal. Ba'hah was being kind to them, they thought. With the breeze lightly nudging them and assisting their paddling, their raft gently bobbed on the waters closer to the clouds. On the fifth day the air suddenly turned still, the clouds unexpectedly covered them and the skies turned dark. Ba'hah stirred her mighty cauldron, churning the waters into a mighty maelstrom. Our ancestors clung on for their lives, chanting orisons to the gods for their safety. They thought that these would be their last days, but as they drew closer to the land emerging in front of them, they saw our islands of Melita and Ga'Desh. Crying their gratitude to the gods for sparing them as they made landfall, as one they promised that, in thanks, they would first build a temple to the gods.

The first temple was a simple affair, made from sun dried bricks and timber. It consisted of only one ovoid room in which the family clan could congregate to worship. A simple stone altar was built at the end of the furthest corner where offerings could be left. Although the first years were hard, in time the village flourished, and it was from these early settlers that our current clan owed their origins.

I sat enthralled as my father recited these stories, eliciting me to ask for more. My father would then shake his head, saying that it was late and maybe another time. My cousins, brother and I would then sigh a collective sigh and retire to our beds for sleep.

One day during the feast of Rabee'ha- when Sem'a rises high in the sky to open her single bright eye to radiate all of her warmth, and Xita'klil sends forth his tears of joy to the new harvest- I wandered through a field of freshly planted maize, pensively looking down and marvelling at the new life of green shoots appearing through the turned earth. I came to an outcrop of stone where the thin soil had vanished and a deep pool of water had formed between the rocks. Peering over to explore, I saw a handsome youth staring back at me and I sprang back in shock. Looking over the rocks at the pool, I saw the youth had disappeared but as I got closer, he reappeared. I pulled a horrible face and the youth in the pool did the same. I poked my tongue out and again the youth copied me. It frightened me and I thought that Xita'Klil had taken my soul to learn my ways.

But what did he want with me?

Puzzled and afraid, I went back home, too fearful to mention this to anyone lest I offend this god and that he would keep my soul, condemning me to live as an outcast.

Our days had become busy with cultivating the fields and planting the new seeds for the next harvest. I sometimes wondered about the strange youth in the pool and again became fearful that the gods were displeased with me. As I toiled, these thoughts passed through my head like a little bird flitting from branch to branch. As these thoughts made no sense to me, I tended to dismiss them to concentrate of the work at hand.

Later, all the people of our village gathered in front of the temple to beseech the gods for a new and plentiful harvest. Dancers in their finest costumes swayed to the chants of the crowd and the beat of the music, which was played on reed flutes and hides stretched over a wooden frame. Young girls with baskets of flowers flung petals in the air, coating the paved forecourt with colour. Each family had baskets brimming with offerings of earthenware bowls, finely flaked flints of a hard and brittle stone which was locally quarried, and carved figurines to be laid at the feet of the High priest. I stood alongside my parents, amazed at this spectacle as I always had been.

I gazed dumbfounded at the impressive building in front of me. It was an imposing structure, indeed designed to generate awe and respect. We were assembling on the forecourt, a large elliptical area immediately in front of the temple entrance paved with flattened limestone blocks. The front wall of the temple façade curved about the forecourt and was constructed from immense vertically placed blocks of limestone, neatly worked so that the faces were smooth with hardly a seam where they abutted each other. Atop of these massive stones were laid horizontal courses of blocks, which raised the height of the monumental façade to that of more than two men. Along the length of its base, a step of blocks formed a bench where some of the older villagers were seated, resting. In the middle of the wall was a single narrow doorway, constructed from two massive carved and shaped upright stones with another carved stone as a lintel. It was obviously created to generate wonderment and reverence. And to me it did!

Everyone fell to their knees as the High priest and Oracle-Iskef- strode resplendent through the doorway with his long dark robe flowing behind him. Around his neck was a jangling necklace of polished animal teeth and clay icons, his face painted with vivid blue and white vertical line and his eyes accentuated with rings of black. He held his hands high.

"Mighty Frott'i, our beloved God of Harvest. May we beg your intercession with Sem'a, god of warmth and light and your kin? Bless these crops about to be planted. May your blessings be on the fruits of our labours and that our harvest be plentiful."

"May your blessings be plentiful," everyone chorused.

Iskef's voice boomed across the forecourt, echoing off the buildings in the village. We all remained prostrate, pushing our baskets in front of us, not daring to look up as the elders walked amongst us gathering up the offerings.

Soon people began rising and getting to their feet. The offerings had vanished and only the flower petals stirred in the slight breeze. Iskef and his elders stood silently and unwavering at the entrance to the temple. Tethered at their feet was a young goat, its halter tied to a tethering point hidden in the paving stones. Slowly, Iskef raised his arms upwards, revealing a short handled dagger made of expertly ground flint and held tightly in his hand. Two of the elders reached down and held the young goat, pulling its head up so that its throat was exposed to Iskef's now descending hand. As the blade came across the goat's neck, Iskef's voice boomed, "may the gods accept this sacrifice at our hand. This is for the good of our people and the produce of their labours."

As the animal's haiya- its life force- slipped away, pools of blood streamed onto the paving stones and trickled into the earth through libation holes to be devoured by the gods.

A hum rolled through the crowd as we watched the goat collapse into the hands of the elders. One stooped and untied the halter. The carcass was then taken into the temple for the ritual skinning and cremation over the temple fire pit in the inner chamber. Slowly and silently the crowds dissipated, returning to their dwellings and communal areas. I stood incredulously staring at the temple, some innate force drawing me towards the portal in the façade.

Suddenly a voice shook me out of my trance, my father was calling, his words seemed to be far off and distant. A hand shook my shoulder and I awoke from my daze with a start.

"Ka'desh," he asked sternly, "are you with this family or not?"

I looked around and saw my mother, brother and cousins all staring at me. Sheepishly I turned and followed them, trying not to look any directly in the eye.

That spring and summer, Frott'i heard our prayers and the weather was kind and merciful and our crops bountiful. It was the best crop yet, my father had excitedly cried when harvest time came. We all eagerly gathered and sharpened our stone knives on whetting stones, following father and the others into the field to cut and reap the corn maize which towered over my small frame. For a short while I was alone with my dreams and memories as the maize swayed in the gentle breeze, until the sounds and voices of my family brought me back to reality.

After the harvest, the village gathered and celebrated with thanks to Frott'i, dressed in their finest clothing richly decorated with flowers and highly polished bone and stone beads. The womenfolk fussed around preparing and serving food whilst the menfolk sat around the gathering area drinking a potent brew made from fermented maize and goats milk. My father had given me some once, but it made my head spin and I could hardly speak. The following day my head pounded as though a thousand drums were being played inside it.

The High priest, Iskef, resplendent in a cloak and cowl made from goat skins covering his face, which was painted in blue and white stripes, and the elders in similar robes, stood impassively observing the festivities. One of the more senior elders stood beside Iskef. Occasionally, the High priest would gesture towards a particular villager and quietly speak to this elder, who would nod as if in agreement, but then continue with their nonchalant observance. At one point I did notice Iskef paying attention to my actions but in silence. It was at this time I first noticed among the elders one smaller person who seemed to be quite different from the others. This person was covered head to foot in a long black cowl seemingly too large for them, and their figure was bent as if they could not straighten up. Although ostensibly one of the elders, this person remained aloofly apart. Intrigued, I promised myself to ask my parents about them later.

Walking away, I joined the other children to run around and play on the banks at the side of the temple, playing a game we called "eet'siq" where one would have to chase the others to try and catch one of them. That person then had to do the same. It required a fleet of foot, co-ordination and cunning. I think I may have had all of these qualities as I was never caught. It never occurred to me then that it would be these very abilities which I was honing at a young age which I would require in a future time, I was just too busy being a child and having fun. With all the rough and tumble of our play, it was inevitable that our good clothing would become soiled and damaged. At the end of the day, I entered our hut covered in the dust of the village, my knees chafed and bleeding and with a huge smile on my face from enjoying all the festivities and frivolity.

"Deshi," wailed my mother, "what have you done?"

I looked down at my dirty and ragged self, noting a few new openings in my tunic, ones which should not have been there.

"Oh, go and wash yourself and then change out of those rags," she said despondently. "I just do not know what I am going to do with you!"

I skipped off to the wash basin and cleaned myself. After changing into my everyday tunic, I sheepishly took the one I had been wearing back to my mother.

"Oh yi..yi..yi!" she said as she shook her head at me. Something inside of me told me that she was smiling at me.

"Omma?" I asked her, "who is the little person with the temple elders?"

She stared at me with concerned eyes.

"When did you see them?" she questioned.

"Before," I replied, "they followed the elders back to the temple."

Mother looked away for an instant then returned to stare at me again.

"Many seasons ago in this village, a baby girl was born to an old lady. This lady should have been too old to be of childbearing age, but the gods thought otherwise. Because she was aged and was growing feeble, after the birth her body grew weaker as each day passed, until her haiya left her and she joined her ancestors. The baby girl was terribly deformed and there were many who said that the parents must have displeased the gods and wanted to cast the child out of the village. The father, in his grief, would not have anything to do with his new child and he left the village in shame. He has not been seen again. I know this as I helped the mother give birth. Iskef and the elders took the child in and cared for her."

"Do you know her name?" I asked.

My mother glared at me for my impertinence but softly replied, "I believe that she is called Anglu, after one of Sem'a's messengers. That is all I will say. It is not to be spoken about again."

My mother then turned her back to me and walked away. I glimpsed her face as she left and I could see a tear drop running down her cheek. As instructed, I didn't broach the subject again.

One morning after the days of harvest were over, my father announced that we would, with some other villagers, make a pilgrimage to the great temple of Jiaganta on the neighbouring island of Ga'Desh. We were all excited as we made our preparations, packing food and clothing ready for the lengthy journey. We would be leaving the following morning. Father told us that it would take us four days to get to Cerkewa where one of the other villagers had arranged for a distant kinsman to row us across the water to Imja, the closest settlement to Melita Island. It would then take us another day to get to Jiaganta where there was to be held a great festival to the gods.

The following morning, not long after Sem'a had raised her sleepy head, we set out on our trek. There was a celebratory-like atmosphere around us as we snaked our way along the well-trodden paths that led along the coastal strip past sleepy villages and large stone temples, not unlike our own. As we passed each village we were greeted by the village menfolk, who waved and shouted their salutations. I was surprised as to how many people father appeared to know. It seemed that he was familiar with every rock, every plant and every person we came across.

Each night we would gather around a glowing fire, under the twinkling eyes of our ancestors, to have our evening meal and then some sleep to rest our weary limbs. Each morning we sleepily awoke to begin another day. We would pack up our belongings, have a light snack, clear the area from our camping and then continue walking along the track. Then, as father had said, on the fourth day we arrived at the tiny village of Cerkewa.

The gods were smiling down on us this day. The waters between our two islands were still and serene, and the rafts were waiting for us as organised. Nervously, we clambered onto the flimsy crafts under the guidance of members of Cerkewa village who would be rowing us across. We squatted in the centre of each raft silently entreating the gods to be merciful and kind. After quite some time, we were drifting into the cove at Imja and eventually onto the short beach. Each of us gave praise to all the gods as we waded through the water to the sandy beach and then into the village.

We stayed as guests in the village, feted and treated as important visitors- none of us could deny their hospitality and friendship. The following morning, after prayers and ceremony, we left our hosts to make our way to Jiaganta.

After what seemed to be many hours trudging along well used paths, we crossed a small valley, and there on the next rise was the magnificent temple we sought. The stories that I had heard must have been true, that it was indeed built by giants long, long ago beyond memory. I thought that our temple at Ta'Shema was remarkable, but this edifice was truly amazing. The walls stood higher than four men, smooth as paste on the outside as if worked from one single stone. The forecourt, although the same shape as at our temple, was much larger, large enough to swallow our entire village and temple. And the temple was as big as the forecourt. Father explained to us that the walls were not a single stone as we thought but made up of smaller albeit still very large stones, and the junctions between each of these megaliths were shaped and fitted together to give the impression of being as one. I remember feeling that Father must have been very wise, knowing this information.

On the forecourt gathered hordes of people from all the villages on Melita and Ga'Desh. There must have been hundreds there, far more than I could count nor even imagine. People stood in groups, some talking and eating, others beating drums and dancing, and others listening to storytellers preaching the ways of the gods. The village High priest casually strolled amongst the throng, occasionally stopping for conversation but in the main observing. Although his dress was remarkably similar to that worn by Iskef, his face was painted with horizontal lines of red and orange ochre. I was about to question my father about this, but he had caught the eye of one of the orators who begged leave of his listeners and approached us.

"Ragel, my friend!" He cried as he hugged my father, "It has been too long. And Omma, you are as beautiful as the day this scoundrel wedded you."

My mother blushed at the compliment and nodded her acknowledgment at the greeting.

"Neputa, my old comrade," my father replied, "yes it has been a long time. Are you with a partner yet or have you remained alone? You have yet to meet my sons Ka'Deen and Ka'desh."

Father gestured proudly to my brother and myself as Neputa nodded to us.

"No, I am still alone, I have yet to find a worthy partner," Neputa answered and then, winking to Ka'Deen and myself, whispered, "maybe I should have become an elder in the temple!"

"But come," he continued, "you must be my guests and accept my hospitality. My home is your home. My hut is not too crowded and is nearby. But first, we must celebrate with the others the bountiful harvest we have had, and the good fortunes of all in the future."

That afternoon and into the early evening we danced and supped to the glory of all the gods. Later in the evening we all sat in our groups around a huge bonfire talking quietly amongst ourselves. I heard a group behind us conversing in hushed tones, but not so hushed that I couldn't make out snippets of their conversation. And that conservation was about me.

I heard my name spoken many times and heard references to the temple at Ta'Shema and Iskef, the Oracle. Then, as the crowds began to rise and disperse, the group behind me rose and their voices were lost in the cacophony of noise which now surrounded us.

As my family followed Neputa to his hut, my mind was a quagmire of thoughts and confusion. What were these people talking about? And how did they know me?

Soon we were making our beds in the hut, spreading a coarse blanket of sheep's wool over a bundle of straw. As I lay down and my head touched my pillow of bundled clothing, darkness overtook me. I dreamt that I was floating, but I was encased within a dark chest. Then the lid of the chest was removed and I was blinded by a bright ball of light above my head. Figures in white hovered about me murmuring to each other in strange guttural tones. Then I was looking down at a grizzled figure stripped bare of any clothing, its skin looking like dried bark on a tree, the white figures hovering around still, inspecting the figure. When I looked closer at the figure's face, I realised that it was familiar, extremely familiar. It was me!

I bolted upright in bed, sweating and trembling.

Prophecy

The dream bothered me – it bothered me greatly. I tried as hard as I could to determine what the gods were telling me, but all I received was silence and frustration. I could not talk to my friends as they would think I was strange, perhaps even stranger than they thought I was now. And I couldn't, as a child, approach Iskef or any of the temple elders. I needed to be introduced by a village elder and there would be little understanding that all I wanted was a dream explained, it would be too trifling. I just needed to work it out myself, if only I knew how. And so my life continued as before.

We spent several days with the families of Jiaganta, being shown around their area like distinguished guests. Very close to the Jiaganta temple was another smaller temple enclosed by a large circle of high stones. They called the temple Sha'ra. We were told that the area within the stones was particularly sacred, that the area was the spiritual home of all their ancestors who had been interred there for more than 40 generations. A massive stone gateway, visible from the Jiaganta temple, led through the stone circle to a smaller and nearly hidden stone doorway leading into a rough-hewn cavern in the rock at the centre. Although we were forbidden to enter, Neputa told us that steps led to an underground temple from which chambers had been cut to lay the bodies of their departed kin. I was immediately reminded of our own sacred burial site at Saffl'na.

One morning after our wakening meal, Neputa sat staring at me curiously.

"Ragel," he said to my father, "I heard a legend from long ago that told of a young man from an island village who would endure to relate the story of our people. There are many in our village who believe that he is amongst us now. I only fear for him if this is so, for he has a great burden to bear – too great for one so young."

"Zibel - rubbish!" My father retorted dismissively with a wave of his arm, but giving me a sidelong glance, "Neputa my friend, you listen to too much gossip. Soon you will be believing that Jiaganta truly was built by giants."

"Ah, Ragel, it is only what I have heard. It is not for me to believe or disbelieve. But the priests and elders all say that it has been preordained by the gods of old."

With a flourish, Ragel arose.

"We have much to do this day," he continued, "I still have much to show you."

When we had all finished our morning chores, Ragel led us along another well-worn path. In the distance, beyond some low rocky hills, I could see the clear and vivid blue of the seas surrounding our islands. As we got closer, Neputa stopped.

"It is this that I wish to show you," he said, as he pointed his bony finger downwards.

Just near his feet a small hole appeared partially hidden by some low bushes.

In a low voice, he explained, "some time ago one of our villagers was banished after a serious wrongdoing. On the death of his partner, he had the need to dig a burial pit in sight of the Jiaganta temple so she would still be with her ancestor's spirits.

But only after he had dug a short way through the rock, he nearly fell into what he at first thought was the bottomless pits of Xi'tan's underworld. Soon, he realised that he was in an underworld paradise. The light streaming in from the hole danced around the void creating a multitude of colours. We now know that it is light of Sem'a that delights the crystals of the cave into all the different colours of the known world."

Neputa then slowly made his way down the hole with us eagerly following. We found that steps had been cut into the rock which made it easier to descend. I soon felt level ground under my feet and looked around in the gloom. An eerie glow wavered from the hole as each of us descended and I felt a cold and damp sensation of something nearby. I was terrified.

Once we had all assembled in the cave, Sem'a's bright glow shone down through the opening. A million tiny dancing, multicoloured lights twinkled from the surrounding walls. The roof of the cavity appeared as if it had flowed and dripped to the floor, forming columns of opaque rock seemingly made up of rings built up until it reached the ceiling. I was awestruck – I had never seen something as beautiful in my short life. Even the twinkling eyes of our ancestors in the night sky would be surpassed by this spectacle.

Neputa stood back, allowing us to revel in this grand display. After several moments, he gestured that we should go. Cautiously we climbed the steps into the glare of the day. Silently and still overwhelmed by the cavern, we walked back to the village.

The next day, was our last full day with our hosts, so we were left to do what we desired. The adults stayed and talked with the other villagers, some rekindling old friendships, others forging new ones. We children, despite being strongly advised to stay close to the village, went to explore the area around the sacred area of Sha'ra. We scrambled around the circular wall which surrounded the temple, often peering where we could into the enclosure to see if any of the temple elders were there. After a while some of the more brazen children climbed the wall and furtively crept closer to the sacred temple. On impulse, I clambered over the wall and attempted to join them. As we neared the stone gateway, we hugged the wall to avoid being seen. Suddenly there was a shout; we froze for an instant, then reactions set in and everyone ran for their lives towards the enclosure fence, however I found I couldn't move. What seemed to be a monstrous hand held firm on my shoulder preventing me from fleeing with my compatriots. I was spun around to face the serious face of an elder. He grabbed my other shoulder with his other hand and shook me.

"What….are….you…..doing….here?" he demanded deliberately and firmly.

My mouth was dry and could only emanate a croak. Just then, another voice broke the silence. I turned my head to see the imposing figure of what seemed to be a giant dressed in a black flowing, hooded robe hovering over me. It was the village High priest.

"Ka'desh?" the voice soothingly spoke, then to the other said, "let him go. He will cause no mischief."

Apprehensively the elder released my shoulders. I attempted to speak but was stopped by the High priest.

"The time will come when your curiosity will be satisfied. It will be then that you may stand among the elders as your peers. But enough for now. We must see you back to your family."

As we approached the village, my father and mother, having been forewarned by the other children, looked at us with concern on their faces. With a wave of his hand, the High priest saluted them and left me to walk the short distance by myself. I was worried that I would be in trouble with Father but it was not to be. Only an awkward silence walking back to the hut. Nothing more was spoken about this occasion again.

On the final morning of our stay, we bade our farewells, extended gratitude to our hosts for their kindness and made our way back along the paths towards Imja. After another three days, we arrived back at Ta'Shema late at night to be welcomed by those we had left behind who were unable to undertake the journey. Although celebrations were mutely planned, we all were too weary from our excursion to partake. As such, we all retired for the remaining darkness. Celebrations could wait till the following day.

We awoke to Sem'a's light streaming into our hut, her warmth radiating throughout. Wearily, we arose to partake in our wakening meal and to do what few domestic chores we had the inclination to do. After some time, we emerged to find many others doing the same, stretching their bodies to release the fatigue from the past days exertions.

At some point, Iskef appeared, like a whisper of wind amidst the growing throng. He held his hands high, stretching his arms over us all.

"Our pilgrims have returned safely," he boomed. "The gods have listened and have given them a safe homecoming. We must rejoice in our good fortune."

Then again, like a breath of wind, he disappeared. Very shortly he returned with the temple elders who lay mats down for Iskef to recline upon.

"Come," he directed, "we must hear news of your travels."

The elders filed behind him to kneel on the mats in anticipation. Iskef gestured to my father to begin.

"Thank you Revered One," my father began, and then proceeded with his monologue, relating how we walked to Cerkewa, what and who we saw on the way, the raft ride across the waters to Imja, the celebrations and hospitality shown by the villagers on Ga'Desh, and the splendours of Jiaganta, Shara and the caves there as well. As my father spoke, Iskef sat watching him closely nodding and occasionally grunting but never interrupting. Once it was clear my father had finished, Iskef spoke.

"And dear Ragel, how was your old friend Neputa?" he asked with a twinkle in his eye.

My father, briefly taken aback, smiled and looked at me then my mother.

"He was well, Revered One, his family also."

Iskef waved his hand, dismissing my father from further duty. Puzzled at the High priest's intimate knowledge of his past, my father stepped back and sat on the ground.

Iskef looked up again. He turned his head and stared straight at me.

"Ka'desh!" he spoke, "What did you find on your pilgrimage?"

Suddenly I had all eyes on me and I felt very, very small.

"Well?" Iskef asked again of me.

"The temple was beautiful," I stumbled, "And they have a temple like ours at Saffl'na. And the cave was really pretty."

My mother nudged me, hissing, "Revered One!"

"It was all really good, Revered One." I concluded.

Still glowering at me, Iskef continued, "pay no heed of any tales you may have been witness to, young Ka'desh. All will be revealed in good time. And good time is what you have."

The High priest arose, followed by the elders. Iskef waited until the elders had retrieved the mats, then turned and strode to the temple, the elders following obediently behind.

We all waited respectfully until we were sure that they had retreated into their domain before dispersing to continue with our daily chores. I remained there for a short time, totally dumfounded as to how Iskef could have known what had transpired on Ga'desh. It was indeed possible that he was merely guessing, as his statements were relatively vague. But then again, he was the High priest, the oracle, the all-knowing.

As each day passed, the memories of Jiaganta slowly dimmed. Each family continued with their cultivation of the fields, repairs to the huts and the manufacture of products ready for the new season's traders.

For us children, life continued much as before – chores, celebrations and more chores. When not involved in family or village errands, we played. However our antics in and around the temple complex grew less and less as we grew slightly older. Our childlike games no longer held interest and other activities gradually became the norm. Some began to take a closer interest in chores around their home. Whether this was by choice or otherwise I could not determine. Others began to learn trades, to learn how to create the fine slip pottery our village was famed for, or how to cut the fleece from the goats and sheep without harming the animals or damaging the fleece, and then to get it ready for spinning, which is what the women folk would do.

As for me, I would select a pick from the tools outside of our hut and head out into the crops to remove the weeds that would choke the crop plants, and to turn the soils between them to prevent any weeds taking hold. This lifestyle permitted me to be lost in my thoughts and allow me to try and determine what life would have in store for me.

It was summer and I had just turned 11-years-old when it seemed that Xita'Klil's plan for me became apparent.

My mother, father and I were in our family hut, my father working his potter's wheel turning new pots for trade, my mother making new clothes from the flax she had recently spun and woven, and I, reluctantly being Mother's model for the clothes.

"What do you want to be when you do Gendus, the man-test, little Deshi?" my mother asked using her pet-name for me.

"I want to be a potter like father!" I replied defiantly.

"And you will be a very good one," Mother responded, "and the gods will bow to your skill."

My father glowered, scowling "only if he does his chores. Have you fed the animals yet, Ka'desh?"

We had 14 goats and 25 sheep which gave us milk for cheese and drinking and fleece for our warmer clothing.

"Yes Father," I fearfully acknowledged. Father was normally a gentle, placid man, but when he raised his voice in anger, the island shook.

Suddenly a bright light streamed inside from the doorway to the hut, silhouetting the figure of a man standing there. We all looked up, startled at this intrusion, and as our eyes grew accustomed to the light we realised that it was one of the temple elders. He beckoned to my father who stopped his wheel, rose and obediently crossed to the elder. Unless one wants the wrath of Iskef, then one must do as bidden. In hushed tones, the two men conversed, and after a short time my father returned to my mother and me. The elder vanished back outside.

"Ka'desh and I have been summoned to the temple," Father said seriously, "Iskef demands to see Ka'desh!"

My mother wailed and through her tears sobbed, "why? Why Ka'desh? Has he offended the gods? He is only a child!"

My father was silent, fearful that the High priest had another, more dire purpose in mind.

"We must go. Now!" He demanded firmly and then promised, "Omma, I will not let anything happen to him."

My mother clung to my hand as I stood and started for the door. I watched in sorrow as the tears fell on Mother's cheeks, but I knew deep inside that everything would be alright. Whatever the High priest demanded was the gods' demand and we would obey without question. And I was certain that the gods would not harm an 11-year-old stripling.

Father and I walked side by side towards the temple and slowly climbed the steps to the forecourt at the temple entrance. The elder waited for us by the narrow door in the centre, bidding us closer. We approached apprehensively, as we villagers were never allowed to enter the temple, that was the domain of the true priests and selected elders alone.

"Iskef will see Ka'desh alone." His voice boomed. Then gesturing to father he added, "and He will speak to you when he is finished."

The elder took my shoulder and roughly pushed me over the step of the raised threshold and through the doorway. Immediately I was in a short and narrow passageway paved with huge limestone slabs and dressed stone walls made of huge limestone blocks shaped and pushed upright so that they abutted neatly onto one another. Above me I could see faint clouds in the clear blue sky. To the left and right were openings covered with heavy hide curtains. As we made our way along the passageway, I noticed another two openings the same as the first two. We went past these as well, until we came to another hide curtain at the end. This curtain was heavily ornamented with embossed spirals and shapes.

The elder stopped me and leaving me in front of the curtain, reached over, took a heavy wooden staff and brought it down hard on the stone floor, sending a resounding noise throughout the temple. He repeated this a second time and then in his booming voice, loudly announced;

"Oh Lord, most gracious. You who are the most wise. You, who can see all. Your servant awaits."

The curtain was pushed aside and I was urged inside. The darkness enveloped me, and as my eyes adapted to the dark, my senses were hit by the smell of wood smoke and burnt dung. I looked around, taking in my new surroundings. As my eyes became accustomed to the gloom, I could see the walls of the apse, all plastered and painted in red ochre - the colour of the afterlife- and the torba, or rammed earth floor hard on my feet. The roof was made of timber logs spanning the top of the walls, the beams now greatly blackened with soot. At the far wall stood a small stone altar, above which was a square hole cut into the wall. I could faintly hear chanting emanating from the hole.

Without warning the chanting ceased and a voice resonated from the hole.

"Come!" It ordered.

I meekly made my way to the altar.

"Closer so that I can see your face, child!" It ordered again.

Suddenly a lighted taper appeared beside my face and I blinked as it blinded me.

"Good!" The voice said with an air of finality.

"You are who you are! You are our legate as prophesied! Through you, our people's names will remain on everyone's lips and their stories will be carved in stone! It is commanded!"

The taper went out, plunging me back into darkness. As I groped my way back to the curtain, I felt a large hand push against my shoulder propelling me back to my waiting father.

Father was then led inside leaving me alone on the forecourt, mulling over what had just happened. The oracle's words bit deeply into my consciousness but as yet I could not comprehend them, only that there was a profound feeling that my life as I knew it had probably just changed forever.

I staggered back into the sunshine, its brightness temporarily blinding me as I caught a brief glimpse of my father being shepherded through the portal that I had just left. I waited anxiously for what seemed an age before my father re-emerged and silently led me back to the family hut.

My mother stood at the doorway nervously watching us approach. She and my father looked intently at each other as unspoken questions were answered.

"It is alright, Omma," my father spoke softly, "we will speak later."

My head was a myriad of questions and possibilities. My 11-year-old brain could not grasp the implications of what had transpired. I only knew that the true meanings would come in time. And as an 11-year-old, time was something I knew I had.

Regardless, the following days passed unremarkably. My meeting with Iskef and the elders only increased my reverence for them. Maybe I would become a priest as well, I often thought. However Father, in his way, curtailed any further continuance of this train of ideas. The monotony of daily chores persisted, starting each morning with the wakening meal and then cleaning up for Mother, followed by tending the crops with Father, chipping at the weeds and thinning the seedlings so that they had a chance to survive, and then any further chores Father desired completing. Then, and only then would playing and socialising with my friends be allowed. We were now at the stage whereby we disliked the label "children," we felt that was a title we had outgrown. "Youngsters" was the title we had now agreed upon, although it was more a compromise than anything else. With this new-found life stage, a period of adolescent curiosity and exploration began.

A friend had told me long ago of a cave less than half a day walk away, where the bones of strange and fearsome creatures lay, creatures which we had never seen before on the island. The cave was called Toba Dweerak, meaning Cave of Sadness, so named by the elders for an obscure reason which we were too young to understand. After pleading with my mother and father for consent to go there, they reluctantly agreed but only on the condition that we did not enter the cave and that we would only observe from the opening. My father sternly warned that dire consequences would occur should this condition be broken, because it was very dangerous in the cave and legends had warned that a ferocious creature still lived there deep within the bowels of the earth. I, along with three of my friends, planned to go there the following morning starting quite early to make the most of the day.

The following morning was bright and warm as we four intrepid explorers, Ahnash, Gisra, Ashra and me, marched across the broken ground and through the rough grass armed with adolescent bravado and a picnic of corn bread and nuts provided by our mothers. We passed several villages on the way, waving and shouting greetings to the inhabitants as we passed, and soon we crossed several craggy hills and thorny valleys to encounter a steep incline leading to a dense thicket of low bushy trees. Pushing the branches and foliage aside, we were confronted by a yawning hole in the rocks. Excitedly, we scrambled over the rocks, oblivious to the cuts and scrapes we were receiving. In due course we were inside the mouth of the cave and ignoring the warnings of our parents, we crawled through the narrow opening. The entrance was surprisingly large once inside, enough to allow all four of us to stand and marvel at the main passage which stretched off into the gloom. As we penetrated deeper, we found the cavity became smaller and smaller until we were crawling on our knees. We were now in almost total darkness, but we found that by keeping to one side of the cave there was sufficient light for us to see ahead. Through the gloom we saw strange shapes protruding from the mud and rock of the cave floor, cautiously we approached to see what they were.

As we crept forward on our hands and knees, my hands gently touched one of the objects and as I slipped my fingers around it, I realised that it was a bone, totally unlike or as large as anything I had seen (or felt) before. Shocked, I fell forward face down into the slimy mud. The others started laughing at my misfortune, plus the fact that I would now be covered in muck. As I cleared my eyes, I peered into the dirt to see the hideous face of a monster staring back at me through empty and lifeless eye sockets, its teeth smiling a grotesque grin, their sharp points appearing to want to devour my very being.

I bolted upright screaming and shouting, hitting my head on the cave roof which elicited another loud shout. My three companions, startled by my reaction, screamed as well. As one, we scrambled as quickly as we could out of the cave.

We sat silently on the rocks regaining our composure. Our legs and arms were red raw from abrasions, our faces streaked in a muddy brown. As we looked at each other, we began to giggle uncontrollably at our appearance and the situation. Only then did we realise the seriousness of the situation and began to speak.

"Why did you scream, Desh?" Ahnash, my friend asked. "You frightened the wits from all of my ancestors."

I explained what I saw and the others dropped their faces to look at the ground, the look of fear in their eyes.

"I saw it too. The legend must be true," Gisra whispered, "We were lucky that we got out in time. We might have been eaten by the horrible monster."

We all nodded our heads in agreement. It was decided that we would not say anything of the encounter to anyone when we returned to Ta' Shema, the least reason being the repercussions of disobeying our parents. We located a small pool at the bottom the hill where we cleaned ourselves and washed our grazes and bruises before our walk home.

Sem'a's brightness was beginning to wane as we wearily trudged back into our village. We bade each other farewell and went our separate ways to our family huts. I pushed my way through the doorway of our home to be greeted by the delicious smells of Mother's cooking. Tonight must have been a special night, as she was roasting some goat which had been slaughtered that day and shared amongst several families to be eaten before it spoiled. Silently, I sat with my family and began to eat.

"Well, how did your outing progress today?" My father asked.

"Good," I muttered between mouthfuls, "saw a lot of people who greeted us."

"Hmmf!" He responded, "and was the monster there?"

He looked up at me with a knowing smirk on his face.

"And was it?" he asked again.

I could feel my hair on my neck bristling and pools of per-spiration beading on my forehead. Suddenly father burst into loud laughter, grinning at me and at my discomfort.

"There is no monster, my young man," he commented be-tween giggles of amusement, "It is only the bones of long gone animals which once grazed on the wild grasses of this land. Fan-tasy has fed the minds of many who explored those caves and that is a reason why they should be left. Let the dead lie peace-fully. Unfortunately, there have been some who have not come out of the caves after venturing in and it has been feared that the cave may have collapsed on them trapping or killing them. That is the main reason we say not to venture in."

By some tacit agreement, my friends and I didn't raise the issue again nor did we desire to go there again. We decided to remain closer to the village unless accompanied by an older person, which didn't really transpire as events would later unfold which would occupy all of the menfolk.

Sometime later during that year, every man in our village including my father was summoned for an audience with Iskef. They assembled on the forecourt of the temple where Iskef and his elders stood waiting. We children observed this meeting from a not so discrete distance where we could overhear the conversation.

Iskef gestured for everyone to seat themselves on the ground in front of him.

His voice boomed loud and clear as he addressed them.

"Menfolk of Ta'Shema. I have asked you to gather here so that we may discuss the future of our temple. It has long become apparent that our village is growing and that this temple, our temple, cannot truly fulfil our needs. Our temple here has been with us for many, many seasons now. It has been part of our village for many generations, much longer than mere folklore can relate. I beseech you then with one question. Can we build another, larger and grander temple which would provide for us for more years to come?"

A loud muttering arose from the crowd as groups of the menfolk gathered to discuss this new proposal. Some became very agitated and had to be calmed by others in their own group. Soon the noise abated and hushed as Iskef raised his arms to restore order and quiet. My father was the first to stand to speak.

"O Great One, how can our village provide enough men to achieve this task? We are only few in comparison to the many required."

A shout of concurrence cried out from the crowd.

"Where would we obtain the stone to build such a temple?" Another yelled, "the stone would need to be quarried from near Cor'din. It would be impossible to move the stones from there to here."

"And who here has experienced the erection of such a project," another interjected, "we are but simple village folk and farmers."

Iskef raised his hands again and the crowd fell silent.

"The villagers of old built the great temple of Jiaganta with their bare hands. They did this many, many generations ago, so many that time has forgotten. Do you think that we are lesser than them, that we cannot do what they have done? Besides, we do have one thing that they hadn't. The numbers of our people on the islands have increased, so that we may call on our fellow villages for assistance. They would be honoured to help us. We can do it, I am sure. We will build a magnificent temple to the gods that they could not help but smile upon our fortunes."

It seemed that the new temple was a foregone conclusion, that everything had already been thought through, planned and executed. Iskef detailed how the temple would be built, to what design, how many men would be required and where the materials would come from. He had conscripted the assistance of a fellow minor priest from Hajarim, Kifa, who had thoroughly familiarised himself with the construction of their temple. He, in turn, had in his company a quiet and astute young man named Gorgo, who had devised a way of transporting and erecting the stone slabs for the walls. A few village menfolk gathered around the High priest and his fellow temple planners, Kifa and Gorgo.

Gorgo explained with a series of markings on the ground, his method of moving the stones and then placing them in their respective position at the temple site. Using teams of men pulling the stones with stout ropes, other rounded stones or rollers about the size of a child's head would be place under the stones which would then move easily, gliding over the rollers. Prior to the stone being set in place, a large hole would be dug, stepped in the side down to the lowest level. When the stone was placed into position at the hole, it would then be levered using large poles until it sat at the lowest level. The stone would then be set upright and the hole refilled, stamping the earth down hard so that the stone would not move.

It all sounded so easy, but as Gorgo and Kifa both stressed, there was still a lot of preparation and planning to be completed first. The first stage would be to level the ground ready for the construction of the forecourt and apses, and the foundation holes for the erection of the walls.

Before they all dispersed, Iskef informed the crowd present that should the temple be progressed then work should begin at the end of the next crop season. My father with some others walked away muttering amongst themselves. It was clear that they did not agree, fully or partially, with Iskef's grand plan. It was something that would not be discussed with me or any others of our family as it was deemed "village men's business" and not for mere children or women's deliberations.

The remaining menfolk slowly dispersed, discussing among themselves this development. It was clear to all that this would take many seasons to complete.

When the days began to warm and Sem'a's light remained longer, work began on the new temple. It had been agreed that it would sit beside the current one almost abutting to it. Gangs of men began clearing and levelling the ground in preparation for the stonework. Three of the village huts had to be cleared, with new huts built for the families concerned. They gladly suffered the inconvenience as it was to appease the gods. The clearing and levelling were going to take some time as the ground was hard and rocky. As there were crops and animals to tend as well, the workforce number waned and waxed according to the village chores required. It had been decided that the work could only be done during the off-harvest season, which meant after the colder time of the year until the middle of the hot period. Outside of this time, life continued as it had always done.

Outside of the daily chores, my friends and I amused ourselves watching the menfolk labouring at the temple site or by taking short excursions to neighbouring villages to meet other friends. Never once did we entertain the idea of returning to the caves. As much as father had dispelled any fears of the known, it was the unknown which we dreaded, and as such declined any notion of returning.

After a few months, the ground beside our temple had been levelled and smoothed ready for the construction of the new one. Some had suggested that the old one would be no longer required once the new temple was completed, but it was decided that it would remain as a sanctuary for the priests and elders. The forecourt was ready for the great flat paving stones to be laid and the layout of the internal structure had been marked by the laying of special stones which had been shaped and painted blue. Unlike the original temple which had only two side apses or chapels, this would have four. Iskef convinced us all that it would allow for better private reflection for he and the elders, allowing a more meaningful dialogue with the gods.

Once the forecourt had been all but completed, the holes were excavated ready for the placement of the huge stones of the outer walls, which were still to be acquired from the Cor'din quarries. Teams of men had been travelling there daily to cut the rock from the quarry face and then dress the frontal surfaces and sides with coarse sand and stone rubbers. In the meantime, others had been preparing the path between Cor'din and our village ready to transport the stones.

There was a chance then, I thought light-heartedly, that I might get to see this grand new edifice in my lifetime.

Manhood

As I grew through adolescence and arrived at the threshold of adulthood, the memory of the cave, my meeting with Iskef and of childhood had faded. Late in winter in my fourteenth year, I, along with nineteen others from our village and Pola- a village near to us- were taken to Hajarim for our Gendus, the initiation to manhood. Once this test was passed, we could own our own livestock, take a wife (provided that we could offer an appropriate dowry) and raise a family. Should we fail, then we were made to continue as children until the following year when it was held again, but made more difficult. In the meantime, we would be shunned by our peers who had passed Gendus as they led their adult lives. My father had explained to me that this trial was more to teach us that village and family came first above all else, and to learn this lesson all candidates were to conduct themselves as one during the test. One cannot live life alone but must be prepared to sacrifice oneself for their brother.

When we candidates gathered in front of the elders on the cliff top near the temple at Su'Riq, they explained the trial to us. We would be in groups of four to lower a canoe down the cliff. We were then to climb down the cliff by rope, launch the canoe into the surf, row the short distance to Fiffl Island and spend two nights with Ba'hah, the sea god. Then and only then were we permitted to row back to the landing at the inlet to Eleq'Gar-the "cave which glows"- to be greeted by our family. The difficulty of the ordeal lay in the timing, as it was held late in winter when Sem'a was resting and blew cold wind from her mouth, and Ba'hah became restless, tossing up great waves onto the rocks to try and prevent us from attempting the short crossing.

At Su'Riq and with three new-found companions, I stood on the cliff and looked down. The wind howled around our freezing bodies and the rain lashed at our skin like stinging nettles. Giant waves crashed upon the rocks roaring in a deafening crescendo then sucking foam and water back to the depths of the ocean. We all were very uneasy as we looked down at that maelstrom, not knowing whether any of us would be injured or even killed. Before we pushed the canoe over the lip of the cliff face, we tied our oars to our backs and a rope to each end of the canoe. With two boys holding each rope, slowly and carefully we lowered it down the rocky face. The wind whipped it around and it was a struggle to keep it steady and not have it dashed to pieces on the rocks. Eventually it was resting on the rocky base of the cliff before being picked up by the next wave which rolled in, drawing the canoe into the surf, pulling at the ropes in our hands.

We tied the ropes around some stunted trees and gingerly descended them towards the base of the cliff. The wind shrieked through the rocks as we all yelled at the top of our voices to one another words of encouragement and direction. In due course we alighted at the bottom and endeavoured to get into the canoe. Teasingly it heaved and bucked like a wild goat until, bruised and battered, we successfully boarded it.

As the seas picked up and tossed our tiny vessel like a kindling stick in the wind, we started paddling frantically, struggling to clear the rocks. Soon we picked up a rhythm with our paddling and were making progress, albeit slowly, towards the tiny isle of Fiffl. We rose onto the crest of a huge wave then came crashing down the other side. Our stomachs churned and heaved with the running swell, so much so that the boy in the head of the canoe suddenly discharged a huge amount of vomitus into the wind, which then sprayed it across us all. Given our circumstances at the time, we were more concerned with making headway and besides, the spray and rain soon washed any detritus away.

After what felt like an eternity, we were staring up at the cliffs of Fiffl. All of the boys had been told that there was a cave in the western face, and fortunately it was the sheltered side. We therefore had little problem landing the canoe on the rocky outcrop and dragging it clear of the water to safety. Climbing the short distance to the cave, we were surprised to hear voices cheering us on.

"C'mon boys!" They cried. "It's all dry in here!"

On entering the cave, we found that the occupants from one of the other canoes had beaten us and were busy preparing a fire from driftwood found inside the cave. Through the shriek of the wind, we could hear faint cries. We peered out of the cave mouth and strained through the spray and rain to see where it was coming from. Through the gloom we could see that one canoe had dashed onto the rocks with the occupants spilt into the water, trying to stay afloat. Without hesitation, I and another boy scurried down the rocks and dived into the raging surf. On reaching the canoe, we found two boys supporting the other two, keeping their heads above water as much as possible. It was plainly evident that two of the boys were injured but we had no idea to what extent. Fighting our way against the current and wash, we made our way back to the rocks where helping hands gratefully pulled the six of us, totally exhausted, out of the sea.

One boy had appeared to have broken his arm, which we inexpertly splinted and wrapped in strips of cloth torn from our tunics. The other said he had been hit by the canoe and had a sore stomach which, unfortunately, we did not heed too much. They both insisted on continuing even though in much pain, and so we all made ourselves as comfortable as possible by the fire, keeping an eye on them.

Before long, fatigue overtook us. Ba'hah howled and screamed around our hideaway and Sem'a roared and thundered against the rocks, but little did we hear. We all slept soundly.

During the night, Bu'sa took the boy with the sore stomach to her home.

We awoke to find his poor broken body as blue as the deep sea and as swollen as a well-fed bullock before its ritual slaughter. He had not as much as whimpered through the night and we all felt a tinge of sadness run through us. We made a bier of driftwood, placing his body upon it and leaving it at the back of the cave so that neither Ba'hah nor Sem'a could steal his soul before his mother and father could offer it to the gods. We then quietly knelt and said some prayers to Bu'sa so that his spirit would not be lost and forgotten.

We returned to Su'Riq after the second night, bringing the boy's body with us. Luckily the weather had abated, so some of the adults waiting on the shore paddled over in canoes to bring back those still stranded on Fiffl. The boy's father was waiting for his return and broke down in fits of tears when he saw the wretched body. He wrapped his beloved boy in his shawl and carried him up the cliff to his dazed and upset wife. When we had all gathered on the cliff top, we fell to our knees as one, weeping for the lost spirit taken by Bu'sa too soon. The boy's mortal body could now be taken to the cave cemetery at Saffl'na to be left with his ancestors and to begin the journey to Xi'tan's underworld.

The boy with the broken arm left with his family to go to their village's healer who would reset the arm, tying it firmly with herbs and bandages. In a few weeks, by Bu'sa's grace and with many offerings to Xi'tan, he could remove the bandages and resume his normal life.

As much as the rest of us had passed the test, we all felt that part of the dead boy's spirit had entered us to remain forever entwined with ours. We truly had all become kindred spirits.

I asked the others his name. They said his name was Suh'la. I whispered a silent prayer for his soul.

After three days of mourning, my family and I made the short walk to Saffl'na. Suh'la's kin were standing forlorn on the forecourt of the small temple. I had been here once before when I was very young when my nannu- my father's Father- passed on to our ancestors, but I had not been permitted to enter the temple. The small temple we could see was a gathering point for the families of the departed, and where the body would be blessed and dusted with red ochre before being taken into the main temple which lay beneath the ground's surface. The underground portion of the temple had been carved out from a cave long ago. Using only the same tools we now used, bone and flint, they fashioned a beautiful image of one of the surface temples from the rocky walls of the cave. It was here that the bodies of our kin were laid when they departed this life, so that their souls may be taken by Bu'sa to her home.

The local village temple elders stood at the entrance doorway to the underground temple with High priest behind them. They all wore long leather robes, their faces partially hidden behind black hoods, their sombre faces painted in red ochre with orange spirals on their cheeks. The structure which we could see appeared to be a much smaller version of the temple at our village, but as I got closer, I realised that the entrance doorway led to a set of steps going into the very bowels of the earth. My body tingled with fear, I thought that we were going to meet Xi'tan.

Suh'la's family menfolk carried his body on their shoulders, covered by the skins of 20 foxes and woven with hawk's feathers. They carried him through the entranceway and down the steps. We all followed in silence until we were in a large cavern, the walls carved by the ancients to emulate the temples which were above ground. The temple elders stood in a line in front of a carved wall with niches behind, their heads bowed and chanting softly. Father whispered that this was called "the Holy of Holies", a very sacred place. Their voices echoed strangely within the confines of the cavern and soon the whole throng of us were chanting with them, becoming louder with each chant.

"Suh'la! Suh'la! Suh'la! Suh'la!"

This was to help his soul find its way to the home of his ancestors.

Suddenly a voice boomed resonantly throughout the cavern, its origin unable to be pinpointed.

"Suh'la! Akba ana istint tal'la Akba!"

In the tongue of the ancients, this means, "Suh'la! The spirit is with the Gods' spirit."

Suh'la's body was then taken by his father and given to the elders, who carried him inside one of the niches of the "Holy of Holies". It was there, we were told, that he would be laid to rest among the spirits of all of our departed families.

As we turned to depart, I felt a hand on my shoulder. Startled, I twisted to see who it was. My family were ahead of me. A temple elder gently squeezed my arm and bending down to me quietly spoke in my ear, "Ka'desh, your time will be soon. You will again be called for by the Oracle of Ta'Shema and you will do his bidding. This you must do without question. Only then can you fulfil the prophecy."

I now became afraid of what was expected of me. Memories flooded my mind of an earlier exchange with the High priest. I still could not comprehend fully what the Oracle had then told me. I wondered if Father knew, and if he did, whether he would or could explain to me. I decided that when the opportunity arose, I would ask him. I slowly made my way back to the sunshine.

Outside the sun blinded me as I sought out my parents. When my eyes had adjusted to the light, I found them sitting in the shade of a tree with my brother, Ka'deen, eating some corn bread my mother had packed in her little carry bag. As I got closer they offered me some, but as hungry as I was, I was unable to eat anything as my stomach churned with my new-found knowledge.

"You look troubled, Ka'desh." My father said calmly. "Did the ceremony upset you?"

I looked at my father enquiringly, looking for something on his face that would tell me that he knew.

"No. Nothing's wrong." I replied, "I think that Suh'la's spirit was troubled but now is contented."

I half-heartedly took a bite of corn bread and chewed on it, its coarseness and sweetness taking my mind to other places.

Ka'deen eyed me with a mischievous look in his eye.

"I think Ka'desh might be in love. He has got a girlfriend." He teased.

My father cuffed him lightly about the head and he went quiet.

Father then spoke softly to me, "Ka'desh, you will be puzzled. But whatever may happen, it is your destiny and it has been prophesised. As much as it grieves your mother and me, we are joyful that you are the chosen one."

At that point, we all stood and walked in silence back to our village.

Two weeks later, my brother's revelation came into being when a beautiful vision came bouncing into my life.

She was of one of the other families in our village and I had known of her since we were both very small. I hadn't seen her for some time, and it was only now that I saw her as a blossoming young woman who made my heart pound like a drum whenever I saw her. She came knocking gingerly on our door to see my mother to be taught the weaving craft. I was the only one there at the time and I gasped and stammered trying to answer her. Her soft and flawless features complemented her long, flowing blonde hair. She giggled softly at my clumsiness and asked if she could enter.

"Of course!" I blushed, regaining my composure. "But Mother is not here. She is in the field gathering wheat and corn for our store."

"That is alright," she replied coyly. "I can wait and then you can tell me about yourself. I have known you for a long time and your name is Ka'desh. My name is Nee'sa."

I blushed again, at once recognising her from a distant memory.

"I haven't seen you for a long time." I said, adding, "I thought that you may have left the village promised to someone outside."

"No," she responded, "my mother had me inside while I started the woman's pains. But now I am ready to go into the world again."

I looked at her again and I could feel the redness of a blush developing once more. She took my hand gently, saying, "it's alright, Ka'desh. I will not embarrass you. But I would be pleased if we could see each other again."

I nodded, unable to speak. Her boldness overwhelmed me and, in a moment, I was besotted.

That night as we sat in the Sem'a's fading twilight, Ka'deen saw the twinkle in my eye and the lightness in my step and commented privately.

"Has Ka'desh found his soul mate? You are like a moonbeam dancing on the grass."

"I think that I have," I replied. "She is the most beautiful thing that I have ever seen."

At that point, Father stepped over to us, having overheard our conversation.

"Ka'desh, you will get such ideas from your head. It is not for you to be on this path, and you will not deny the gods," he demanded.

Puzzled, Ka'deen looked at me and then at Father questioningly. Father just turned and walked away.

"Ka'desh? What does he mean?" Ka'deen asked.

I shrugged my shoulders, not fully comprehending either. That night I had another disturbing dream.

I felt as if I was floating, my hair drifting in front of my eyes. Everything appeared blurry and as if a mist surrounded me. Suddenly a strange face appeared and slowly moved directly in front of my own. The eyes were wide open but unseeing, the face bleached white and expressionless. Gradually it drifted away and out of sight. I opened my mouth to speak but only bubbles formed to float out of my mouth and past my eyes. It was then I realised that I was under water. I started to panic, trying to grab anything near me to help me float to the surface. A skin used to carry fresh water floated past me with a small pocket of air inside, I grabbed at it but it was out of reach. I could feel my mouth filling with water and I started to cough as I felt a pressure on my chest. The water around me began to get darker. The heaviness on my chest became greater until everything was black.

I awoke to realise that I was still in my bed, snuggled in the skins keeping me warm. The dream bewildered me as it had no meaning to my life in the village. My freshest memories of water were of my Gendus when I, with the others, had to risk our lives in order to come of age. The monsters of my dream, however chilling, were a dire warning from the gods, but I could not understand their counsel. I eventually drifted back to sleep to more tranquil reveries.

Nee'sa and I saw each other frequently over the following weeks, though only in passing. When she called for her lessons with Omma, we would greet each other cordially as I made excuses to leave. As I walked down the path from our hut, my heart would sink as if I had lost a lifelong soulmate. Father did not interfere at this stage in our relationship as he was employed with many of the other men building the new temple.

As the days passed, I could no longer disguise my feelings for Nee'sa, each time I saw her my mouth would go dry, my tongue would knot and my thoughts jumble. I thought that I had upset one of the gods and that they were punishing me. When I spoke of this with my mother, she softly chided me in her motherly way.

"Oh Deshi! You are in love. Your body has found its soulmate," she crooned, "But you will not let your father know of this. You must never tell him!"

"But why?" I asked.

"You must put this from your mind," she responded, "Only your father knows why. You must not question this."

At that point it was left, never to be spoken of again. Torn, upset and heartbroken, I walked away. What was it that the gods had in store for me? I reasoned that it must have been important for the High priest to have carefully chosen me from all others to fulfil his prophecy.

And so life continued in the village. The new temple was slowly taking shape, the ground had been levelled and the pits had been dug ready to place the enormous blocks of stone. The stones had been cut and roughly finished in a quarry a day's walk from our village, and were ready to be hauled to their new location where they would be shaped and smoothed prior to their installation. Large piles of spoil from the levelling process were added to other rocks from the fields to be used as a filler between the stone walls. As Iskef had predicted, other villages near to ours offered a labour force as their own needs dictated. I, along with many others, was now excited at the prospect of a new place of worship. I was sure that the gods would smile long and hard at our offering to their greatness.

My relationship with Nee'sa initially continued as one of friendship, which puzzled her at first, but she grew to accept it. Often we would walk side by side along the many paths in the hills surrounding our village, talking absolute nonsense and laughing at each other's antics. We talked about mundane things such as the weather, the harvest and sometimes our families, but more often of each other – our dreams and aspirations. Although Nee'sa spoke freely about herself, I always felt constrained, remembering the words of my father and the Oracle. As much as I strongly desired, some innate fear of an unknown consequence prevented me from following my heart and asking Nee'sa to be my life partner.

Early one evening when Nee'sa and I walked along the path between our villages, she took my hand and stopping and turning to me, she kissed me gently on the cheek.

"Why are you distant to me, Deshi?" Nee'sa asked earnestly, "I know that you like me. What is it you cannot tell me?"

I took both of her hands in mine and looked into her eyes, so intense, blue and beautiful.

"I cannot tell you as I have been sworn to secrecy," I replied despondently, "I want to be with you till the end of our days - I really do. But the gods have said that it is not to be. You are my life and my soul and it tears me apart to say this; as friends and companions we must stay. That is my fate as foretold."

"What do you mean, foretold?" she asked.

I became angry. Not at Nee'sa but at the High priest and the elders of old.

"It seems that someone, an Oracle somewhere, maybe an ancestor, maybe the gods themselves, have decreed that my life has been chosen to fulfil the words of the gods, so I have to live my life according to rules which they have set." I scowled. "It has never been my choice and it is a path that I would gladly pass to another, someone more worthy than me."

"Oh, Deshi!" Nee'sa despondently answered, "Does that mean that we can never be as one? That we can never be wedded? It will be difficult for me to be friends only. I want more from you."

"We can remain as friends only," I responded, "The elders, Iskef and even my father will see to it. It has been written in the sands of ages."

I had already divulged more than I should and I could feel my heart shredding apart as we left each other on that path. As we walked away from each other, I saw teardrops falling from her eyes. I must admit that I felt very much the same.

My brother took a wife during the last harvest season and was now enjoying his own life. My friends had grown and now also lived their own lives with their respective families. I continued doing my daily chores as I had done for years, occasionally helping my father find good quality clay for potting and the infrequent chance to make something with my own hands.

My peers were mystified at first at my apparent celibacy and my seeming lack of matrimonial interest with Nee'sa. After some friendly banter and teasing, they grew to accept what appeared to be my choice. Ka'deen was naturally suspicious of my sexuality but never spoke of it in public or private. He, like the others, accepted that my decision was mine alone and that it did not seem to displease the gods. However, I felt like a beast with a heavy yoke around my shoulders. I could no longer live my life as I would like but would have it preordained by the gods for all eternity.

The heavy responsibility which had been thrust on me must have showed itself to my parents because early one evening as Mother prepared our evening meal, Father took me outside to speak to me.

"You have not been yourself lately, Ka'desh." He admonished gently, "what is it that worries you so greatly?"

I just looked at the ground, sweeping my foot back and forth in the dusty earth.

"Is it the path that the gods have chosen for you?" He continued. "Most people do not know what path has been chosen for them until they have already lived that path. All of our destinies have been selected by the gods to allow us to use our own abilities for our betterment, and they keep the knowledge of that path very close to their hearts. You, on the other hand, have been told where your destiny lies. That in itself is an honour which no other can take from you, you should accept and hold it proudly. Where your life will lead, I do not know. All we can do is guide you as well as we can. Be proud of your heritage and know that we your family, the temple elders and priests and our ancestors will be with you every step of your way."

A tear ran down my cheek as I looked up at my father.

"But why me, Father?" I sobbed, "Why me and not someone else. I cannot do what they expect of me. I am not worthy enough!"

My father wrapped his monstrous arms about me and clung to me tightly. I felt his lips give the top of my head a soft caress before he released me. I threw my arms around his waist and squeezed him tightly, then stepped back to wipe the teardrops from my eyes. When we entered the hut, Mother looked questioningly at Father then to me. No words were spoken. No words needed to be spoken. Silently we sat and ate our meal.

Apprentice

One balmy evening late in the warm season, an elder came to the hut once again. I was outside sitting idly on some rocks whittling at a piece of bone with a flint.

"Ka'desh," he uttered softly to me as he sidled up to me. I looked up at him, both startled and questioning.

"The time is here," he continued, "you have a few moments to gather any personal belongings you wish to have with you and to say your farewells to your family and then come with me."

On hearing the voices, my father, mother and brother came out of the doorway of our hut. They looked at the elder, then at me with a look of resignation. I slowly arose and shuffled over towards them. Parting to allow me to enter the hut, I went inside and looked around, confused and at a loss of what to do. My mother bustled past me to gather my few meagre belongings and bundled them into a tight ball tied with leather straps. As my mother and I busied ourselves, my father stood in the doorway with a concerned look on his face.

I picked up the ball and slowly scuffled towards my father. He stood barring my way, so I stopped and looked up at him. Uncharacteristically, he spread his arms wide and enveloped me in a firm and loving embrace.

"Take care, my boy," he said quietly to me, "may the gods smile on you, whatever may come."

I then felt my mother hugging me tightly from behind and felt her warm lips kissing the top of my head.

"Mind your manners," she sobbed, "and remember your kin always."

With tears welling in my eyes, I silently nodded to them and turned to follow the elder.

We walked towards the old temple, passing the new temple forecourt which had been almost completed. The great flat slabs had been laid and were now ready for the final finish, where they would be rubbed smooth and flat. Beyond the forecourt holes had been dug and made ready for the enormous and dressed stone uprights to be set, mounds of excavation debris neatly piled behind each hole.

This, I thought to myself, will be absolutely grand. I wondered if then our village would host pilgrims visiting our temple.

My meandering thoughts must have slowed my progress because I was curtly chastised for lagging behind. Almost tripping on an uneven stone, I scurried to catch up.

We did not pass onto the forecourt of the main temple, instead we followed the wall to enter the priest's enclosure through a high gate. Inside the enclosure there were four huts – smaller than our family hut but still relatively large. One had two erect stones intricately carved with spirals, birds and animals, and across these two stones, a flat stone sat as a lintel with an elaborate carving the form of which I could not determine. This was obviously where the High priest resided. Behind one of the other huts was a small lean-to which appeared to have only recently been constructed. Inside was a rudimentary bed and a receptacle for personal belongings.

"This is where you will live during your stay with us," the elder explained and then continued, "You will have your meals with us - the elders and High priest- and you will be expected to carry out additional chores as we may require. In the meantime, your time this evening is your own. You will commence your apprenticeship tomorrow at first light. Sleep well, young Ka'desh. The morrow will be a long one."

As it was late in the day, I had already partaken in the evening meal with my parents, so when the elder left me to my own devices, I began to unpack my possessions and make my accommodation as comfortable as I could. Soon the light began to fade, and I struck a flint and lit a small taper I had found on top of the shelf for my belongings. As I climbed into my bed and blew out the taper, and before weariness overtook my eyes, I took stock of my situation. My mind was in turmoil as to what was expected of me and why. As I drifted off to sleep, I began to imagine that my life was probably going to be that of a temple elder.

The first few days with the elders were very leisurely. Each morning at first light I was awoken to witness the elders perform their daily rituals and, after the awakening meal, assist in cleaning the huts and around the perimeter of the temple. Once these chores were complete, I was left to scour with a coarse brush the many vestments the High priest wore, scrubbing the dust and grime from the soft leather and coarse wool. There were times that Anglu joined me to silently assist and, when I tried to engage a conversation, I was met by a pair of steely eyes staring at me from beneath the darkness of her cowl. She would then vanish into the darkness of the temple leaving me even yet more inquisitive.

Just before Sem'a rose to greet us on the fourth day, Iskef strode out of his hut and made his way towards my lean-to.

Bending over and peering in, he boomed, "follow me!"

Startled, I awoke from my slumber and rubbing the mist of sleep from my eyes, I quickly tidied my area. Emerging from the lean-to, I saw Iskef waiting patiently outside.

Abruptly he turned and strode off, with me scuttling behind wondering whether I should protest my lack of sustenance that morning. He brushed through the high gate of the enclosure to approach a hidden door in the rear of the temple. From inside I could hear the dull murmuring of chanting as the elders praised the gods for another day, to give them thanks for this land and the life we led. This was called the Filhodu – the morning thanksgiving.

My stomach grumbled in hunger as it realised it was not going to be sated.

"Wait!" He ordered, and I nervously stood outside. Moments later Iskef reappeared and marched with me obediently following, back to the enclosure. As he approached the portal of his hut, I apprehensively paused.

"What are you waiting for, boy? Come!" Iskef commanded. I nervously followed through the doorway into the darkened room.

"Sit!" He ordered once more. I peered into the gloom and knelt on the hard turf floor. Iskef sat on a pile of skins opposite. On a large platter were slabs of bread, fruit and nuts and beside, a large gourd of water. Iskef gestured for me to eat. Appeasing the grumbling which by now had become noticeably louder, I partook in the meal.

"This will be the first of your lessons." Iskef commented as he tore a large piece of bread in half, "you are to remember everything you are told. It is imperative that you do this if the prophecy is to be fulfilled."

He then stood up and paced the floor before stopping in front of me to stare into my eyes. As his gaze fixed on mine, he squatted down onto his haunches.

"This is what the signs have told us," he continued, "you will leave the village and your travels will be long and dangerous. You will not return. You will have personal loss and grief on this journey, but you will face your fears at every corner and your faith will prevail. Remember your past, control your present and guide your future. Your destiny is our destiny. Our story will only be told in the stones and dust of history. Your story will answer the riddles of those stones. I cannot tell you how to commemorate our story as I do not know. This is one of the mysteries which your journey will answer."

He paused for a moment for me to digest what he had just said, then he continued speaking to me, explaining the stories of the creation of our world, that everything is linked together by the gods. Every thought and every action has been directed by the gods. As such, when we pay homage at the temple, there are many rules and rituals which he, the High priest and Oracle, and the elders must perform to appease the gods. The people of the village, since the gods allow some latitude in thoughts and beliefs, are not required to enforce the rituals as vigorously. There is, he stressed, a requirement that everyone have unconditional respect and reverence to all the gods at all times. If there is not, then only misfortune will fall upon those and their family who transgress. It seemed like an age later when he rose, beckoning me to do the same.

"Have you any questions, young Ka'desh?" he asked of me.

"None that I can think of," I replied as my mind reeled with this newly given knowledge. Visions of the High priests of Giaganta and Saffl'na flashed across my mind and immediately a question arose.

"Please if I may," I pleaded, "I do have a question."

Iskef glared at me, a wry grin appearing on his otherwise stoic face, and nodded.

"Why do the High priests paint their faces?"

"Ah! A good question." Iskef answered then adding, "the colours and how they are painted embody the priest's village. You will have noticed that I have vertical lines of blue and white. These are the colours of our clay from which your father moulds his pottery. It is merely the clay on my face. You will have seen the priests from Giaganta and Saffl'na who have red and yellow. Their paints are made from powders traded from afar of which the red powder, or ochre, is used by the priests to bless the mortal remains of our departed kin. The red symbolises the dust of the earth, Bu'sa's flesh, to which our bodies return and our haiya joins that of our ancestors. The priests of Giaganta and Saffl'na have the red because of their association with the burial sites within their temples."

I nodded my head, though not really comprehending fully. I thought that maybe it will come to me in time. As Iskef motioned for us both to rise, he glowered down at me, his eyes piercing mine. His voice serious, he spoke.

"You have met Anglu, our young protégé. Be tender with what you say to her and how you treat her. She has faced many monsters and has yet to face many more. Many of these will be very painful for her to experience. Her trials are not unlike those that the messengers of the gods endure in their battle to communicate the god's message to us. This is why we call her Anglu."

I followed Iskef from his hut, and as he walked to the temple, I made my way to my lean-to to prepare myself for the evening meal.

That night I sat quietly with the elders, ready to eat our evening meal of coarse bread, oil and dried nuts. My mind was filled with a myriad of questions to which I could get no answers. Anglu sat on a mat beside mine, her face still shrouded by the black cowl.

One of the elders pointed to me saying, "Young Ka'desh. You will say the blessings on the food."

As pious as my father had been in our home, we had never partaken in blessing our meals.

"We thank the gods for granting us this meal," I stumbled, "And we thank them for our good company."

A chuckle arose between them as one of the elders replied, "I suppose that will please them. I see that we have our work cut out for us, young Ka'desh."

With a wink in my direction, he bowed his head and consumed his meal. Once finished dining, the elders and Anglu got up and retired to their own quarters leaving me to clean the meal area and dishes. Not that it bothered me any, it was something we children were expected to do at home after each meal. Once finished, I returned to my lean-to totally exhausted and ready to go to sleep.

The following day after a light awakening meal, Iskef summoned me again, this time to meet him in the temple forecourt. I found him there, standing straight and tall in all his majesty. Without turning, he greeted me in a gruff but friendly voice.

"A pleasant morning to you, Ka'desh. I trust you slept well? We have a lot of things to cover and discover today," and with a flourish he commanded, "follow me."

We walked away from the village along a stone fence enclosing a field of newly cut barley. The sweet smell of the crop accosted my senses as we stopped at the mid-point of the wall.

"Do you know who built this wall?" Iskef asked.

"N..n..no I don't!" I stuttered uncharacteristically, "it has always been here. I suppose it was built by the ancients."

"Yes, it has always been here for us," Iskef said softly, "As it was for my father and his father. But it has not been here for all time. At some point, it had to be erected. Our history is like this wall. Some may look at here and now and say it has always been thus, but at some time past we were not here and, still, at some in the future again we will not be here. That is the riddle of our time. Our forebears at some distant time ago began their life on our island so that we may live in our time, and we have lived peacefully with one another during that time. In order to continue our lives so that our children's children may live, we must continue to live peacefully. That is why our people do not carry tools to harm another person. These tools of hurt and harm are forbidden. Some may be tempted to use our tools and craft to cause hurt and death and we cannot allow that to happen. It is up to the temples to calm and protect our people. I can see that our people will come to an end sometime, though not in our own lifetime, and our ways of life will be lost forever, only the dust and stones will be able to tell any story."

"Who built our temples?" I asked him.

"The ancients built them long, long ago," he replied, "long after the first pioneers. At first, they built simple places in which the community worshipped. They were humble mud, brick and thatch huts, but in time the people outgrew them. As the huts were shaped as a fowl's egg, then the bigger temples had rooms the same shape. It was thought that this shape was a sign given by the gods, so it was to be continued. The temples then were first built from local stone and so the walls could not be too high. It was then discovered that some of the large rocks in the cliffs and hills could be easily split to create a large section of wall. The walls could then be higher and stronger. It took many very clever and wise men to construct the new temples, but they knew that they would outlast mankind themselves. I know that you have been with your family to Jiaganta and have seen with your own eyes the splendour of that place. No, it was not built by giants as the legends state. It was built by man. And it has stood the test of our times having outlived many, many generations."

"Will our temples and stories still be told many years after we have joined our ancestors?" I asked Iskef.

"Ah! Little Ka'desh!" Iskef crooned, "only the sands and waters know the answer to that question. This is why the ancients have appointed you to carry that story, so that the story will never be lost to time."

We sat together in silence for some time, pensive in our thoughts. Mine were still a quagmire of questions which would probably never be answered.

Iskef turned to me abruptly.

"What is it that you would like your life to behold?" He asked.

"I wanted to take my life partner and to grow old with her. Maybe we could have had many children to bless our home," I earnestly replied, "But I now know that dream is one that cannot be fulfilled."

Suddenly tears welled in my eyes. I was overwhelmed with emotion as recent events caught up with me.

"I am not sure that I am worthy of this task, oh Great One." I stammered.

"Worthy you are, of this I am absolutely certain." Iskef soothed. "The ancients' choice would not have been foolhardy. You will do well, my boy. And you will do your people proud."

In silence we returned to the temple enclosure. I sat in silence during the evening meal, digesting what Iskef told me. The other elders knowingly nodded their acknowledgement of my presence and dined in silence. On completion of my chores, I went to my bed and slept soundly.

Each of the following days at the temple was much the same. Rising just as it got light and now joining the elders for the ritual Filhodu. Although they were spoken in the tongues of old, I soon knew the prayers and rituals by rote. Each was a chant of the same phrase over and again, but each time given a different inflection to emphasise another aspect of our daily lives.

After the wakening meal, I accompanied Iskef to a new location each day, chosen for its relevance to that day's lesson. Each lesson had as much to do with temple life as to my life in general. I was slowly growing to appreciate the deeper significance of the lessons as to my destiny. Each one taught me a life lesson, each life lesson was a choice and each choice would lead to my vocation.

Each day I would encounter Anglu and by now I could faintly discern her mouth curving into a smile when we met. We still had not spoken with each other yet. One afternoon, as I was about to enter my lean-to, I felt a presence behind me. I turned to find Anglu standing close by. She had now pulled her cowl partly back so that I could see her face. At first, I was taken aback, repulsed. Her mouth was only a slot in her face, but it was curled at the corners into the smile that I had only seen glimpses of. Her left eye was pulled down to the same level as her nose, her right eye totally absent, covered by a closed eyelid. Embarrassed, she drew her hood back over her head and spun around to leave. All feelings of repulsion suddenly left me, this was my companion of the past days, the one who would kindly smile at me every time we met. Compassion now became my emotion.

"Wait," I wailed, "I'm sorry. I should not have felt like that. You are my friend. I was just surprised."

At that, I shut my mouth, fearing that I was digging myself a deeper hole to fall into. Anglu turned and stretched out her arms. It was only then I noticed that one arm was only a stump with short malformed fingers, the other fully formed but the fingers were fused together. I reached out, taking both of her hands in mine and gently squeezing them. It was then she uttered her first words to me.

"Tunk oo." She murmured, and then retreated to her own hut.

Months passed, and each day of each month had been a gruelling journey of teaching me the ways of the world, not just our village. Each day, Anglu would appear by my side as my companion for at least part of the journey. In some respects we had become kin – she becoming the sister I had never had, me the family that she had been denied. Each day she exposed more of her true self, becoming more confidant, engaging in conversation (albeit rather stilted at times owing to her disabilities) and no longer wearing the cowl over her head to hide, but proudly revealing to the world her deformity. At times when we were left alone, we would try to converse, and as difficult as it was, we managed to develop a kind of sign language to supplement her lack of ability to talk clearly. I was sure that our antics during our "conversation" would seem rather comical to an outsider looking in, but we did not care. Our companionship was all that mattered to us.

One day Iskef came to my lean-to as the other elders went to the morning ritual.

"Ka'desh my son," he spoke gently, "it is time that you rejoined your family. I have nothing more I can teach you. Your lessons must continue with you alone, as you live your life. The ancients have chosen your path and this you must now travel alone. Learn from your experiences each day, trust your instincts and follow the examples of your elders."

Then on a lighter note he continued, "we can only applaud you for what you have achieved with Anglu. We have not seen her as happy and full of confidence as we do now."

He stretched out his grizzled hand, in which he held a small figurine of a grossly enlarged and seated female form. It had been carefully carved from an animal's bone and had a thin cord of leather threaded through an eyelet at the top.

"Take this, young Ka'desh, and wear it always around your neck. This is Bu'sa, our mother goddess, protector of families. She will protect you on your life journey. I will not wish you good luck as luck has no part in your journey. However I will say good blessings on your future and may it lead rewardingly."

Without giving me a chance for thanks and farewells, silently like a wraith he strode back to the temple.

Replete with the new found knowledge I had gained over my time in the temple, I walked unsteadily back to my family's hut. There to greet me with a beaming smile and open arms was my mother. Without a word spoken, we hugged, before long being joined by my father. For several moments we were wrapped in each other's arms just joyful that I was home again.

Once we had composed ourselves, my mother took the small figurine hanging around my neck in her hand.

"This is the earth goddess," she repeated to me, "she who protects our families and who guides our departed to Xi'tan."

"Wear this well," she continued soothingly, "never lose it and always wear it well. Your people will always be by your side whilst you wear it."

Extremely puzzled, I went to bed pondering the hidden meaning in my mother's words.

I awoke to the sounds of voices. Peering into the gloom of the hut through sleep squinted eyes, I caught a glimpse of a lithe figure with flowing blonde hair. Nee'sa! I sat bolt upright and jumped out of bed my heart racing. I stared at her in the dim light, in anticipation.

"So, are you becoming a priest?" She asked teasingly.

"N..n..no!" I blushed, "no I'm not. I was at the temple learning the ways of our people."

That was diplomatic enough, I thought.

"I know." Nee'sa said softly to me, "but we were worried that you would."

"Enough!" Mother interrupted, "Deshi, have something to eat and then you may go and spend your time with your friend."

That too was diplomatic, Mother, I thought.

Nee'sa was full of questions. What did I do in the temple? What did it look like in the temple? What are the elders and Iskef really like? Where did I sleep? And eat? What did I learn? I answered as best I could without disclosing some of the more confidential aspects of the temple that I had either been made privy to or that I had noted and been sworn to secrecy about. When I broached the subject of Anglu, Nee'sa suddenly went quiet.

"What is wrong?" I asked her, concerned.

"I have been told that she is an evil one, cursed by the gods," she muttered through clenched teeth then adding, "it has been said that under that dark hood of hers she has the features of one of Xi'tan's heralds, and that one look from her would wilt and wither the poor unfortunate she had chosen."

"They are only village tales," I replied, "made up by those who know no better, those who are threatened by a person who is different. Anglu is different from us but only in the physical sense. Underneath her tortured exterior is a very gentle and lovely person."

I then proceeded to describe Anglu, her physical disabilities and her personality. The only curse she had had was that her birth was difficult because of her physical deformities. Given different circumstances, she could have become an integral part of our village, however knowing the prejudices of some, I knew that that would never happen. When I finished my discourse, Nee'sa leaned over and gently kissed my cheek.

"You, Ka'desh, are a kind, perceptive and tender person, and that is why I will always love you." She whispered into my ear. I brushed a tear drop from her cheek as she said this and hugged her, cuddling her loveliness and longing for her continued companionship. I knew now, ever more certain than in the past, that this would never be.

As we ambled arm in arm up the pathway, we talked about more mundane things such as the weather, what had been going on in the village and what progress had been made on the new temple.

That soon became apparent as we reached the crest of the rise. There beside the old temple, a large flat area- seemingly larger than that of Giaganta- had been gouged out of the earth and rock. A tall façade of large stones, squared and smoothed, had been placed and fixed in their anchoring holes and set to curve about what would soon be the forecourt. The stones stood the height of two men and atop them were the beginnings of several courses of horizontal stones to take the height of another two men. In the centre of the façade was a large portal framed by massive stone blocks, smoothed and shaped to fit perfectly within the other blocks. The structure was obviously far from complete, as this was expected to take quite a few more seasons.

I just stood there with my mouth agape in awe at what my village, my people, could achieve. This was indeed a temple worthy of the gods. Regardless of the cost to our village, with menfolk taken away from their normal chores, the depletion of our stocks of food to feed the vast workforce gathered there, and the deprivations of the womenfolk and their families, we would be more than compensated by the majesty of the structure.

It would be still many years before the temple would be finished. Farm life and family still took precedence. Some years the crops would be very lean with little or no rain to replenish the water storages, the dirt drying out and the crops withering in the dust. Other years the rains would come in a torrent, drowning the crops and almost doing the same to the inhabitants of our islands. The wind would howl and whip its way through the huts and whistle and moan through the naked stonework of the new temple. At times like these all work stopped, the workforce returning to their own villages. Irrespective of the weather, Iskef would be seen in his dark robes, the tempest howling about him, at the temple shouting incantations into the wind.

In a way I sympathised with him and from that my respect for him grew yet stronger. This was his dream, his mark for prosperity, but I also felt that although the temple would endure for ages, the privations and the energy put into its construction would be forgotten with time. It was this aspect that saddened me, and tragically and paradoxically, I would not see its completion.

Journey

During the time of Sem'a's warmth and in my 19th year, I was taken once more to the High priest. One of the elders came to our family hut late one night, waking my father and mother and informing them that it was time for me to depart.

"You must take as few of your possessions as possible," the elder ordered, "all you need will be provided."

Mother quickly gathered a clean tunic for me and surreptitiously spirited some pieces of goat's cheese, dried meat and a piece of bread in among its folds. This was then rolled into a small ball with a loop of cord to enable me to carry it over my shoulder. I just stood and watched the proceedings in the dim flickering light of the fire, totally stunned and shaken at this turn of events. My father grabbed my arm and pulled me into his embrace, bringing me back to reality.

"My boy," he said to me, "no I mean my young man. You must take care when you are away from us. You do the gods bidding and will make our ancestors proud. Take care, my son. May our love be always with you."

A tear rolled down my father's cheek. It was only at this time that I realised that I had never seen my father cry before. I must admit that I was close to doing the same, it was only the bravado of my youth preventing me. My father released me from his hold, only to have his arms replaced by those of my mother.

"Deshi, Deshi," she sobbed, her tears wetting my face and hair, "my little boy has grown up. Be careful in your undertakings, my Deshi. I love you with all my heart. We love you with all our hearts. May the gods be generous to you and may you never forget us, our people."

It was then that the floodgates opened and I too burst into tears. I clung to my mother tightly, my chest too tight to breathe, my mouth too dry to speak. Eventually I found my voice.

"Farewell Mother," I croaked, "Farewell Father. I can only try to do what I am asked. I do not know whether I will succeed, but whatever may come, I will never forget you, the people of Ta'shema and everyone here. My love for you will never cease, be it in this life or the next."

The elder and I left for the temple in silence. I knew that this would be the last time I would see them all! I felt the tears starting again so I fought hard to hold them back. I did not want Iskef seeing me in this state of what I perceived to be weakness. We walked along the path past the construction site of the new temple. The standing stones stood as a silent silhouette of a mute sentinel, shrouded by a thin ghostly mist.

It will probably be finished by the time I get back, I absentmindedly thought to myself, then berating myself when Iskef's voice echoed in my mind repeating what he once said, "You will leave the village and your travels will be long and dangerous. You will not return."

I took in all the sights, smells and sounds that my mind could accommodate as I followed the elder ever closer to the main temple. Knowing that I would not return, I needed something tangible to remind me of my home.

When we mounted the temple forecourt, I saw three men, not of our island, talking in a vaguely familiar tongue. One of the men appeared to be deep in conversation with the High priest. They all fell silent as soon as they became aware of my presence.

Iskef glared at me, holding up his hand to silence me as I approached.

"Ka'desh, you will leave with these men. They are from a distant land much like our own. There you will learn their trade, language and customs, but heed this and heed it well. You will never forget your home. But you will not return. This is to be your destiny as it has been foretold."

Staring at me with his deep-set eyes, Iskef looked at me questioningly. He then stooped down to me and spoke softly.

"Ka'desh, you have excelled yourself beyond our expectations. You make your parents and ancestors proud. You have made Anglu proud, and she sends to you her deepest wishes and respect. It has been you who has brought her out into our world, no longer hiding behind dark shades. She is now content with what the gods have endowed her with and it is because of you that that is so. She asked me to extend her gratitude to you for this, and for you to always remember her as she will you."

With an air of finality, Iskef turned abruptly and disappeared into the darkness of the temple.

A coarse hand grabbed my arm and I was led roughly away. The three men talked among themselves in their own tongue as we walked along the paths in the moonlight. The language they spoke was not dissimilar to our own so I could understand scraps here and there. Not a word was spoken to me, perhaps a grunt when we stopped or a low growl when we resumed. Obediently I followed them as we made our way past villages and temples, sleepily lost in the low mist hugging the ground, until we reached the harbour at Cor'din. There, a large watercraft floated just off the shore. It was nothing like I had ever seen before, curved low in the middle but with each end pointing high out of the water, crested by the figure of a corpulent female form at one end and the figure of a ferocious animal at the rear. It appeared to be made of timber bound tightly together in some fashion, the sides fused as one piece and covered in a black tar. At the front on each side was painted an enormous eye, white with a blue border and red dot in the centre. I could smell the odour of stale fish and I could hear the vessel creaking in the low swell. A small but curious crowd had assembled on the rocky shore.

We waded through the water, reaching the side of the vessel where strong and calloused hands reached behind me to lift me up and over the side of the craft. My three new companions clambered over the side and bustled off to perform their assigned chores. I was left to sit on a soft skin at the end of the vessel, puzzled at this new event in my life but intrigued by my first time on something larger than our own rafts. The craft lurched lazily on the small waves rolling into the shore. The gentle rocking and pitching made my stomach grumble somewhat, causing me to nearly vomit. My head grew light and my brow became saturated with perspiration, I had no idea what was happening to me. A thought passed that a curse had been cast on me. I sat still with my head in my arms and soon the feeling passed as I got distracted by the undulating sound of voices, soft and muffled, wafting across from the shore, my name being clearly spoken a number of times.

One of the crew- the one who spoke to the High priest at the temple- seized a rope hanging from the front of the boat and started heaving it in. Soon he was dragging a heavy stone weight tied to the end of the rope. He looked up at me and noticed my curiosity.

"Ankra!" he said, pointing to the stone. I nodded back at him, only barely comprehending.

Soon the men pulled large poles from along the sides of the craft and began to use them to push it through the water. Slowly the group on the shore became more distant and as I watched them, they drifted away returning to their lives, the distraction of my leaving no longer there. I watched the shoreline grow ever more distant as we drifted lazily out of the inlet. We passed village after village along the shore until we came to a series of three headlands jutting out into the bay. A high hill dominated the land on the other side of us, a small temple visible on its crest. Beyond that yawned an open mouth of water between two other tongues of land. As we sailed closer, I could see the ocean churning its waves towards us, the cap of white foam spuming in the soft breeze. Again, the boat began lurching up and down and side to side riding the churning waters. Again, my stomach stirred with the motion threatening to empty its contents down my front. I dashed for the side and unceremoniously hung my head to gush forth the former contents of my gut. I wiped my mouth with the back of my hand, sneaking a furtive look around to see if I had been observed. I looked away embarrassed as I saw a trio of the crew chuckling as they stared at me.

We passed out of the protected waters of the bay and into the open waters of the ocean, and the land which was once my home slipped further behind us. Almost immediately a beehive of activity started on the vessel. A tall frame of two poles lashed together, each pole securely tethered to each side of the vessel, was slowly hauled up and secured by strong ropes. Another pole laying across the vessel was then heaved up the frame. A large sheet of leathered animal skins bound together was tied to the pole and the ends flapping at the bottom were secured to the sides of the vessel. Soon, the soft low gusts of breeze were captured in the skins and it soon billowed out, slowly propelling the vessel through the waves. Soon the boat was moving smoothly and sedately through the still waters of the harbour towards the gap between two arms of land. As it drifted through the gap, the ocean swell lifted the front up only to crash in a flurry of spray into the next wave. Startled by this sudden and unfamiliar motion, I sat up and almost fell over as the boat plunged once again into the swell. The nauseous feeling began to overcome me again as I scrambled to the side to empty my stomach into the churning water. In the pale light I watched the men scurry about performing a multitude of tasks, each of them completely alien to me. With the breeze now picking up, the skins filled and billowed, propelling our fragile craft through the water. Unable to settle the uneasy feeling in my stomach, I stretched out on the skins looking up at the dark sky flickering with the bright eyes of all our ancestors. Eventually my body became accustomed to the pitching and tossing of the vessel on the ocean's waters and I soon fell asleep.

When I awoke, I felt the now familiar sensation of moving, albeit a slow motion, in all directions. A cool breeze brushed gently across my face as I arose to stretch my aching limbs. I was fascinated as I looked around me to see nothing but water, as the raft lifted and fell then rocked sideways on each passing wave. The position of Sem'a in the sky had me guess it was around midday. As we lifted to the crest of yet another wave, I realised that we were very close to land, but this was no longer Melita. On the horizon I could see the peak of a hill higher than any I had seen before, almost as high as Sem'a's bright eye. At the crest of this peak, a pall of smoke and fire, like the fiery furnaces of Xi'tan, burst into the sky.

Tired, confused and frightened, I stared at this plume of smoke. It must be Sem'a's warmth burning the top of the hill because it is so tall, I mused. That is what happens to our skin if we stay too long in her sight during the hot days of the year. So it must be so!

"Mongibello!" a voice behind me grumbled. I turned to see that it was the man who had hauled the "ankra" onto the boat.

"Huh?" I asked bewildered.

"Mongibello!" He repeated, pointing to the hill. I nodded, not really understanding whether that was the name of the monster spitting fire into the sky or the name of the hill. My mind flooded with a multitude of questions, but I feared that a language barrier would make them difficult to understand. I had had my very first encounter with a mountain, albeit very distant, and I stared in awe at its vast majesty.

The vessel approached a sandy cove, dominated by near sheer cliffs rising high above and behind. Atop the cliffs I could make out the shapes of huts and the smoke from burning campfires. I wondered how anyone could get from the shore to this settlement, until I detected a path twisting its way up the precipice. At one end of the beach rose an elevated outcrop towering much higher than the village. Nestled at its apex I could discern what appeared to be a stone structure, which I assumed to be some form of temple much as it would have been in my home country.

Amidst a clamour of voices and the clattering of gear being moved around, I became afraid that we wouldn't stop and our flimsy craft would shatter itself on the approaching shore. I took one more glimpse at Mongibello in time to see a flash of red fire issue from its summit, then a ringlet of grey and white smoke swirl and gyrate upward into Sem'a's home. The gods knew that I was here!

Hordes of people waded into the water as the men threw loops of strong cord towards them to drag the craft up onto the sandy beach. Two of the men jumped over the side of the craft, the sea only coming to their waist, and helped the others haul the vessel clear of the water. The man who remained on the craft started gesticulating at me what I first thought were threatening signals, but then I realised that he was motioning for me to jump over the side. As I did so, I was surprised at the softness and the whiteness of the sand between my toes. It was totally unlike the gritty and golden sand of home.

People gathered around me, curious eyes watching as I walked gingerly up the beach towards the prominent figure of a man standing directly in front of me. He obviously was held with some reverence, as all the others maintained a discrete distance and avoided his penetrating gaze. He was very tall and was dressed in long, flowing and colourful robes. He wore a large headpiece made from the head and antlers of a deer. Around his neck he wore a necklace of small bones and teeth, each highly polished so that they glistered in the sun. Around his waist he wore a thong of rope under which was tucked a gleaming reddish gold dagger, the likes of which I had never seen before. His face was old- not through age, but through wisdom- gnarled and withered like an animal skin left outside for too long. His eyes were deep-set, peering out through sockets darkened by ash. His nose, long and sharp, offered prominence to his weathered face. He stared at me as I apprehensively approached him. He offered a scrawny and bony hand towards me as I knelt in front of him. Terrified, I looked up and felt his hand, cold and rough, on my head. He uttered something incomprehensible then beckoned for me to rise and follow. Obediently, I did so.

We walked in silence through the low sandy dunes of the beach and up a steep path cut roughly between dark rocks, looming up the cliff-face from the foreshore. Every now and then I sensed a vibration in the ground beneath my feet. I was sure that Xi'tan was trying to talk to me.

O Lord of Darkness, I thought privately, please be patient with me. I will give you my privations as soon as I can.

The ground shook again. The man in the robes and the others paused momentarily, looking to the sky murmuring something, then proceeded up the path. The path was made from beaten earth and shaped stones, creating steps which clung precariously to the steep cliff. The climb seemed exhausting after the period of constant rocking on the raft, but soon we broke through a copse of trees into a small village, not that different from home. As I gazed around, I noticed that small fires were burning in each of the huts, the smoke gently rising into the warm morning air, the smell of cooking drifting with the smoke. Beyond the village, a vast field of crop was growing, the long stalks gently swaying in the breeze. A hand gently prodded me in the direction of one of the huts where one of its occupants was standing at its low and narrow doorway.

"Vente!" A voice grunted beside me. Surprised at this intrusion of sound, I turned to the source of the voice.

"Mita Ghadoh!" The voice spoke again and a large, calloused hand pointed to the young man standing in the doorway. He was a lean young man, sinuous but with an unnaturally dark skin. He had a deep, penetrative stare through deep-set eyes, as he turned his finely chiselled face towards me.

Not understanding completely but with foresight, I pointed to myself, saying, "Ka'desh!"

The young man called Ghadoh nodded and indicated for me to enter the hut. Inside, I was "introduced" to an older man who I could only assume at the time to be his father, and a woman roughly the same age as the man. The man motioned for me to sit beside him as the woman hustled a bowl of food for us all. Ghadoh ladled some of contents of the larger bowl into a smaller one then handed it to me. I looked at the contents and discovered that it was some form of meat stew with what appeared to be vegetables. Whatever it was, it was tasty and filling since I had not eaten in nearly a day and my stomach was grumbling more than Mongibello.

After the meal, I was offered a bed of animal skins and covered with course cloth, and gratefully I fell into a deep sleep.

I was dreaming. I was floating over fields of white. I was cold. Shivering, I looked down and could see through a thin mist, two men running up a rocky hill. They appeared to be hurt, as one was limping badly and was carrying the other on his shoulders. A number of other men appeared to be chasing them but were far behind them. Soon, daylight invaded my dream as I awoke, my mind a tangle of thoughts as I tried to unravel its meaning.

The dream lingered in my thoughts as I rubbed my eyes. Momentarily I panicked, confused as I took in my surroundings and then realising where I was. The hut was round and on one side, where I was, there were several low wooden frames, with beds of skins and cloth much like what I had just slept in. In the middle of the hut was a hearth for a fire, its embers still smouldering and its smoke drifting upwards to a hole in the centre of the roof. Opposite to where I sat was the entrance to the hut, the narrow doorway shielded by a heavy curtain. I was alone but could hear voices outside.

I arose, and walking to the doorway, stooped and went outside. Near to the doorway the tall man in the robe was conversing with the father, Ghadoh, and one of the men from the raft – the one who spoke with the High priest at my former home. They turned towards me when they noticed my presence.

"Ghadoh you have met, and he will teach you our ways. Ghadoh has lived with your people and knows your language, so you will be able to speak to him," the raft man said to me in my tongue, then gesturing to the tall man, added, "and this is our Oracle and High priest. You will call him Veritani."

He ignored the father.

Ghadoh entered the hut. I followed and we sat on cloth pillows next to the smouldering fire. He reached over, grabbed a log of wood and threw it onto the fire in a shower of sparks.

He turned to me speaking with a strange yet familiar accent, "you have been sent here to learn our ways. I am to teach you. Do you understand?"

I nodded my head in understanding. I had a myriad of questions but felt that there was a lot of time to ask them.

The ground shook, rattling the implements and crockery hanging around the hut. Again, the ground shook, this time more violently, throwing us to the ground.

"Mongibello grows anxious," Ghadoh explained. "She has not been happy for a long time. Her rumblings are getting worse."

The earth heaved upwards, throwing us around. The wooden pole in the centre of the hut bent drastically, causing the roof to start to collapse.

"Quickly! Outside!" Ghadoh commanded. We only just cleared the doorway as parts of the roof began crumbling down. Outside was a scene of chaos with huts in various states of collapse, women and children screaming in panic and cracks appearing in the dried walls. I looked up at the mountain in shock. Thick clouds of grey, white and black smoke shrouded the summit reaching high into the sky. It was as if the gods of the underworld were angry and were creating sparks through the dense smoke over the sky above the mountain. Great rivers of flames flowed down its flanks devouring everything in its path.

Horrified, I could only imagine that this god of the mountain must be more powerful and fearsome than Ra'barak, the thunder god. This god could move the ground and burn everything to a cinder with its breath. I hoped that it was not me whom she was angry with.

Cowering together, partly in fear, we waited for Mongibello's rumblings to quieten. After what appeared an eternity she quietened, and stillness once again descended upon the village. Veritani appeared as if from the dust, creating a commanding presence as he paraded masterfully around to restore calm and peace. He began calling the menfolk to begin repairing the damaged huts, at which Ghadoh and I took part willingly. Veritani then turned to the womenfolk and children, directing them to gather the animals and fowl now running amok, free from their enclosures. In a relatively short time order was completely restored, albeit for the few huts still damaged, but teams of menfolk were still rectifying this issue.

As evening drew near, Ghadoh beckoned towards me and I followed him to a rocky outcrop, high on the cliff, overlooking the water. It was very near to the temple I had seen on my arrival. On the distant horizon, I could see dark grey clouds menacing the otherwise tranquil setting.

"You! Me!" Ghadoh hesitantly started, "we will come here every day, where I am to teach you the ways of our people! I do not understand the reasons why this is to be so, only that it has been decreed by the gods of long ago."

He continued, "the people who live here are called the Siculi, and their legends tell the story of a time when the wells and streams dried up, the earth was hard and no crops would grow. The people were dying as there was nothing to eat. One family built a raft of fallen logs, and crowding all their belongings and what livestock they could carry, sailed it to the edge of the waters where they were not seen again. In time, there were rumours of people living on an island very near to our homeland. Our ancestors built more rafts and sailed off to search for these people. After many days on the water, they found your islands and it is from that time that we have become kin again."

He gestured his arms around him.

"We live in these huts with our clan, our family," he continued. "Our gods are like your gods. The god of water is Sydon, the god of land is Hera, the god of sky is Cielo."

I nodded, amused in my own way at their names for the same gods whom I was accustomed to. A breeze began blowing, soon picking up to become a stiff wind. The rain clouds loomed closer and the rumblings of Ra'barak's anger rolled away into the distance. Spots of rain began to fall, intensifying to a heavy downpour. Ghadoh and I quickly got up and found shelter under a low shrub.

As we settled and watched the rain falling around us, my mind flooded with curiosity.

"Ghadoh?" I asked, "how did you know that I was coming?"

"I have been told that the priests of ages long gone told of your coming, before you and I and even the village-folk were born," he answered.

I contemplated that for a while, striving to put everything into context but unable to do so. I mulled over what Ghadoh had told me thus far and certain things became clearer.

"You were not born of this village, were you?" I asked intuitively, changing the subject.

"No," Ghadoh replied deep in thought. "I was born in a distant land like you but, at a young age, was caged as a farm animal by cruel people from great settlements far beyond my home, in a place they called Uruk. I was treated like an ass to work for some important man. They said that he was their king, their ruler. His rule was absolute and his word was never to be broken. If you broke his word, his law they called it, then it was punishable by torture or even death. His home was bigger than anything I had seen, hundreds of rooms all beautifully furnished with the richest furniture and the finest cloths they could find. His house was surrounded by other homes much the same. Many thousands of people lived in this community. My own people lived in large settlements but nothing as vast as what I saw with my own eyes. They worshipped a God they called Barl who was the god of all that is wrong with creation. They said that if you did not worship him, foul deeds would befall you."

Intrigued, I asked further, "Can you tell me about where you were born?"

A tears welled in his eyes as he continued, "I lived in a land which bordered the gods' blood of life, a river of bounty which we used to travel from community to community floating on rafts made from a grass called papyrus, a river which we bathed in to cleanse ourselves in the god's beauty. Each year, at the God's command, the river would overflow its banks to enrich our farming soil so that our crops were always bountiful and lush. Our leader was born of the gods to dwell with mankind, to ensure that we all have a passage to the afterlife. This is what I know from what little I remember of my life then. I recall that my mother was beautiful, her smile would light the darkest night and she was very gentle. My father, I think, was a craftsman, though I am no longer certain. I remember that he often went with our people's leader, Meni, to many of the new temples being built."

After a pause, he continued, "I was playing in the reeds of the sacred river, when I felt coarse hands grabbing me from behind. Then a cloth was placed over my head and I was carried off. I recall being tied to a camel and being dragged through the desert, the rest is really a haze! Eventually, when I was much older, I escaped, and after a long and arduous journey ended up here. Jisah and Grimat, the man and woman you met in the hut, took me as their own son. I have never been back to the land of my birth."

"What is a Ca-mell?" I blurted, "and what is dess-ert?"

"All in good time, my inquisitive one. All in good time." Ghadoh replied.

"How did you learn my people's tongue?" I asked him, my curiosity getting stronger.

"For a time I worked for the boats people, trading to nearby islands, including yours. During one voyage, we sailed to your island with a leader who was inexperienced with your winds. We had to stay at your island for nearly six months until favourable winds allowed us to return. While there, I stayed with a family who lived on the small island near yours, I cannot recall its name."

"Ga'Desh." I replied, "it is called Ga'Desh."

"Yes, Ga'Desh." Ghadoh continued, "I was with a family who lived in a village near to one of your great temples – the one they say was built by giants. The man in the family was very kind to me. His name was Neputa."

I was now speechless. It seemed that my whole life was intertwined and twisted around everyone whom I had encountered.

Several weeks later Ghadoh woke me early and, grabbing some coarse bread and some goat's cheese, dragged me outside. In hushed tones so that no-one should be woken by our noise, he whispered to me, "there is somewhere I want to show you, but it is a half-day's walk. It is a place very special and very holy to our region."

I was eager to learn something of their beliefs and so was anxious to see this holy place. I had only seen the temple on the hill from a distance and had yet to see any others where worship could be practised.

We walked along tracks worn smooth by countless feet, up hills and into valleys. On occasions, someone would wave a greeting to Ghadoh and shout his name. Before long, the track wound through a thick forest of tall trees and up a steep incline. Soon we came to a rocky crag. Ghadoh led the way between boulders until we came to a dark opening between the rocks. Taking a large fallen and dried branch, he wrapped some dried moss and vines about one end, then striking a flint he started the moss burning. Beckoning, he disappeared into the opening.

At first I hesitated, as the overwhelming memory of the cave of Toba Dweerak flooded my mind. Were there any monsters in here that would harm us? I blocked the memory from my mind, reminding myself that it was only an adolescent fear, albeit one which had manifested itself in me and made me very wary. Stumbling behind him I crawled over rocks and boulders, trying to adjust my eyes to the dim, flickering light of the torch Ghadoh held. As we went deeper into the cave, the floor became smoother and the air cooler. Following the twists and turns of the subterranean passage, we eventually arrived in a huge cavern, the roof so high that it could not be seen in the light of the dancing flame. Soon my eyes became transfixed on a sight so beautiful, and so magical that I was speechless.

In front of me on the wall of the cavern were painted figures, different kinds of animals (some of which were very strange to me) and of people hunting, fishing and generally living life.

Ghadoh saw the look of astonishment on my face and as he softly spoke, his voice echoed throughout the cavern.

"These were painted a long time ago, at the beginning of time. No-one knows who the painters were, but they must have been my tribe's ancestors. This cave is our link to them and is held as a very sacred place, we believe that these are their souls, forever painted on the walls."

I was transfixed for quite a while, acknowledging the ancients' haiya forever encapsulated in the figures on the walls. Ghadoh shook me from my thoughts to point to the waning flame on our torch. We made our way out of the cave as quickly as we could, and as we sat on the rocks blinking in the bright sunlight, I spoke.

"They could have been my ancestors as well!"

And with that thought still in my mind, we made our way back to the village.

As we got closer to the familiar surroundings, I heard an unfamiliar grunting and movement in the bushes ahead. Ghadoh suddenly stopped, holding his hand back to stop me in my tracks.

"Wh.. wh..at…" I started to say.

"Hsst! Quiet!" Ghadoh hissed at me, as a wild boar crashed through the trees to stop dead in its tracks in front of us and then glowered, snorting and pawing the ground, its tusks appearing menacingly dangerous.

Without taking his eyes from the beast, Ghadoh whispered for me to remain still. Several long moments passed before the beast slunk back into the forest.

Breathing a sigh of relief, Ghadoh turned to me.

"It is a game of your wits against the beast," he said, then continued, "if you move and you have nothing with you to defend yourself, the beast will surely at least maul you severely, at worst kill you. Give it enough time, it will lose interest."

Thankful and comforted by his words, I breathed a huge sigh of relief and we returned to the village.

Over the following weeks Ghadoh and I were inseparable companions. Each day was another learning experience, being educated in the Siculi ways of life. The Siculi, I was told, believed that they were the original inhabitants of their land, having been there for thousands of generations. Their lives, like the Malti- my people- were intricately intertwined with their lands and all that dwelt there. Their gods were very similar to ours, however there were some peculiarities particularly with regards to Mongibello's grumblings. It seemed that Mongibello was very seldom satisfied and would frequently vent her dissatisfaction at the most inopportune time, as I had recently experienced.

It seemed that although the Siculi villages in this part of their country lived peacefully, the Sicani- who dwelt on the furthest side of the country- believed that they were the original inhabitants and therefore resented the Siculi presence. While there had been relative peace between the two societies in recent times, conflict was always simmering, ready to erupt like Mongibello's fury. This was something which was completely alien to me, having been raised in a land where violence was not only discouraged but avoided as much as possible. However in light of this, I was taught how to throw a spear and armed with a bow and arrow, which Ghadoh taught me how to use. These key skills, he stressed, were essential for survival in his land.

One afternoon, as a gift to celebrate my accomplishments, he gave me a small knife made from a gleaming reddish gold material which he called copper. He explained that it came from a rock found in the mountains, and that the material could be melted on a very hot fire and moulded into shapes. In this state it was still very soft, and required heating and beating to make it much stronger and able to be sharpened to a fine edge. Despite Ghadoh's advice, I quickly learnt that the gleam soon diminished to a dull brown if the blade was not kept clean and sharp, but once restored, I was taught how to remove the skin and clean the entrails of small animals ready for roasting and eating. In no time I became exceptionally adept at all these new-found talents.

There were many times when I was left alone to explore the village and its environs. It was at these times that I would look up at the rocky promontory where the temple lay, curious as to its association with the village. Whenever I questioned Ghadoh about it, he either avoided the question or gave a very guarded response. One afternoon I had been left to my own devices and decided to have a closer look. The path leading to the temple was wide and steep, at times there were rocks laid down to form steps where the rise became too steep. After a strenuous hike up the hill, I found myself on a flattened area in front of a series of massive stones set on their ends into the ground in a circle. Within the circle, I could make out the shape of a squared stone sitting in the centre. Each stone in the ring had been carefully shaped with flat sides and sharp edges. Between the stones there was a small gap, large enough for a person to walk through, though it was obvious that this hadn't been the case as there was no wear on the ground from foot traffic. As I scanned the area in front, I noted an ornate trilithon consisting of two orthostats with a heavy lintel across the top. Rich decorations of spirals and squares were carved up each vertical block, with the lintel carrying carven figures of deer, cattle and bears. The space between each vertical was as wide as a man's outstretched arms and therefore was evidently the main entrance. Curiosity drove me closer, and as I was about to cross the threshold of the entrance, a loud shout shook me back to reality. Looking around, I saw Ghadoh with Veritani and a host of other village menfolk. None of them appeared to be very pleased with my explorations.

Veritani grabbed my arm roughly and dragged me around to face him.

"This is a sacred place," he sternly scowled at me, "only those who have been indentured in the arts and mystics of the ancients may enter. Those who defile its sanctity are to be flung from the temple to the rocks below, their lifeless bodies to be devoured by the ocean and its creatures within."

"Why did you come here, Ka'desh?" Ghadoh asked.

At first I was speechless, shocked at the way Veritani manhandled me and annoyed that I had never been warned or told that this place was off limits.

"I'm sorry," I pleaded, "I was not to know. I wanted to see if the temple is the same as ours back home."

Dismissing the other villagers, Veritani pulled me to one side then beckoned for Ghadoh to join. He gestured for us to sit on some convenient rocks nearby.

"This," he explained, "is a sacred place. It is where the founder of our village first fell to his knees to give thanks to our gods, for giving him guidance as to where his people may settle and prosper. The temple was built around the very stone that his tears of thanks fell upon. There are very few individuals who may enter its hallowed space. It is where the newborns in the village are brought to be indoctrinated and welcomed into our society, and it is where the dead are brought so that their souls may bear witness to the ancients before their interment in a tomb. I am sorry that Ghadoh had not informed you of this prior, but it was my unfortunate decision to advise him not to."

I nodded my acknowledgement, at last now knowing what my mind questioned. Veritani and Ghadoh escorted me back to the village in silence. The subject was not broached again.

Weeks turned to months, and soon I was mostly accepted by the villagers as I turned my hand to assisting in daily chores and offering my hand to the almost ceaseless maintenance of the huts. My grasp of their language was mostly complete and as such, Ghadoh now spent less time with me - his job was nearly complete. There were one or two small groups of younger men who shunned me, even to the point of being overtly hostile at times. One, a young huntsman not much older than me named Nirrox, accosted me as I walked alone on the path from the beach.

"Where have you been, Little Weed!" He taunted.

Not wanting confrontation, I replied diplomatically to that effect. After a gruff grunt, he pushed past me almost knocking me off my feet, sarcastically adding, "maybe you should go back to that bullock dung of an island which you were spat from!"

At first I was unable to understand their hostility. With the exception of these youths, the villagers were very friendly towards me and I was very much accepted into their village family. There were many others, much my own age, with whom I would socialise as well, particularly a pretty girl by the name of Vilucia. She was dark and lithe with long flowing black hair and eyes like the stars at night.

Nee'sa had been my first and one love, but she was denied to me both by providence and distance. It was hard now for me to ignore that the passions of a new love interest were rising inside me. The words Iskef had spoken to me at what now seemed an age ago still resonated in my head, but I could not disregard where my heart and mind were attempting to lead me. It was these thoughts which conflicted with the hostility shown to me by Nirrox.

Emotions in turmoil, I continued up the path to the village. I turned my eyes to the heavens, beseeching Xita'Klil to show me the way he wanted me to take. That night, I remained quiet and aloof and lost in my thoughts. This was not lost on Ghadoh and his adopted family, although nothing was said.

That night I had another dream. I dreamt that I couldn't breathe, my mouth and gut filling with water. Above me was a tangle of rope, timber scraps and lifeless bodies. I tried to swim up to the surface but something around my ankle held me down. As I slowly drifted towards darkness, my ankle was set free. As I turned to see what had freed me, I could see Ghadoh's face smiling at me as it slowly drifted away into the murky distance. I awoke in a start, sweating profusely and shaking. I looked over at Ghadoh in the half-light to see his chest slowly rising and falling as he slept. It was only a dream, I admonished myself! After a short time, I drifted back into a dreamless slumber.

The following morning, I sat silently picking over my food. My mind was in turmoil going over the troubling dream I had had the previous night.

Jisa and Grimat looked at each other briefly then to Ghadoh.

"Something is troubling you?" Ghadoh enquired of me.

I glanced at the three of them and, looking down, replied, "I had a bad dream last night which disturbs me greatly. It is one of many which I have had, and I cannot comprehend what its meaning is. I have asked the gods for their guidance but it eludes me. I am unsure that I am truly worthy of the trust placed in me by my family's High priest."

Jisa glowered at me, a concerned look shadowing his face.

"You must speak to Veritani. He will have the answers you desire. I will arrange an audience with him."

Jisa quickly arose and moved silently out of the hut.

Later in the day I was summoned to meet with Veritani. Gingerly, I made my way down the cliff path to the beach where I had been ordered to go. Veritani was waiting on the beach, his back to the cliff and hence me.

"You wished to see me, Revered One," I softly spoke as I approached behind him. His right arm shot up, his hand spread as he turned on his heels towards me. I instantly fell silent.

"Your dreams trouble you, young Ka'desh?" He quizzed. I nodded my head.

"Your dreams are your future, young Ka'desh. It is what you do with your dreams which will become your destiny, and your destiny has been predetermined by the prophets of old. One day, you will be able to put your dreams into your story and it will all be clear," Veritani uttered softly, adding, "it will only bewilder you and distract you if you attempt to understand your reveries individually. It is only when they are seen as a whole that they will make sense."

With that, Veritani strode away to the cliff and climbed the path, leaving me to puzzle over the riddles he had just posed. The only thing which was clear to me was that I would never see all of my dreams whilst alive. And it was that part which concerned me greatly.

Lost in thought, I stumbled up the path to the village. As I reached the crest, Nirrox and his friends blocked my way.

"I thought I told you to go back to your dung heap," Nirrox snarled. His friends sniggered at this.

"Maybe you need some encouragement," Nirrox snarled again as he pushed against my chest.

I noticed that two of his companions had stolen behind me, blocking any escape. He pushed again causing me to stumble backwards.

I heard voices behind me calling, "Little Weed! Where's your dung heap? Where are the rest of your family, crawling around in all the shit?"

The jibes continued, interspersed with howls of derisive laughter. I continued trying to step back to avoid them, edging closer and closer to the edge of the cliff. In due course, I completely lost my footing, flailing my arms as I fell over the lip of the rock face. Frantically I clawed at the rocks and shrubs, trying to catch anything which would slow my fall. Hands bleeding and my body bumping down the steep slope, I glimpsed the world spinning around me, dizzily turning and turning, until my mind went black.

I sensed that I was still, and my arms, head and legs hurt.

Can you feel pain, I thought, if you are dead? I tried to lift my head and open my eyes, but an agonising pain prohibited me. I tried to call out but my voice did not come, only a feeble croak issued from my mouth. I heard voices in the distance but could not make out what they were saying, and eventually they faded completely. I slipped back into unconsciousness again.

It was night-time when I opened my eyes. I found that I was trapped on a boulder jutting from the cliff face, my tunic caught on a wiry shrub growing tenuously there. I tried calling again but could not find the strength to do so. I drifted into blackness again.

I sensed, rather than felt, something around me and the pressure of the shrub and boulder being released. I could hear muffled voices above me getting closer. Hands reached under me and gently laid me on firm ground. I opened my eyes to see the smiling faces of Ghadoh, Jisa and Grimat looking down on me.

"The gods be praised!" Announced Ghadoh, "He is still with us!"

Hands picked me up again and gently carried me to Jisa and Grimat's, hut where I was laid down on a bed of skins.

My three extended family members all sat staring at me. It was Ghadoh who spoke first.

"You have been very lucky. It was only by chance that Nirrox found you. You owe him your life."

Jisa then said, "Veritani will be here soon to tend to your injuries. We pray to the gods that you are not too badly hurt."

I closed my eyes. I was dumbfounded that Nirrox had turned this to his advantage. I could never have imagined the animosity and cruelness shown to me by him and his friends happening in my homeland, and never would anyone have the temerity to benefit from another's misfortune. That was not the Melita way. It bespoke disharmony with the gods, who would seek recompense.

I felt spindly fingers shaking my shoulders and I awoke to see Veritani beside me. He waved his hand in dismissal at the others and they exited out of the hut. Veritani's thin hands slowly kneaded and pressed over my body, concentrating on the areas where I experienced pain and on the mobility of my arms and legs. There was a deep graze on my thigh oozing blood which he lightly padded with a swab of moss then bound in leaves and strips of leather. He then lifted my head and pressed a mug of pungent liquid to my lips, encouraging me to drink it.

Standing up, he glowered down at me and spoke in his deep resonant voice, "you have the fortune of the gods smiling at you, young Ka'desh. In time your body will heal. And also in time, I will determine the cause of your misadventure and bring to task those responsible."

And with a wink, he turned and left with a flourish.

It was many weeks before I was able to re-join the village in chores and life in general. Jisa and Grimat fussed over me as I healed. My leg wound mended leaving a light scar, but my limbs took time to regain their strength. Vilucia came to visit me many times whilst I was invalided in my bed and our friendship grew stronger. Her gentle smile and girlish twitter when she laughed amused me, although deep down she reminded me of Nee'sa. When I was able, I walked around the village with Vilucia holding my arm to steady me as we greeted and spoke to the villagers we met.

At first Nirrox and his companions kept their distance, but as my wounds healed and I became more able, so their presence became more obvious. At first it was the gentle shove as they pushed past me as before, then to more hostile acts such as open and confrontational aggression. As much as I was hurt emotionally by these acts, I ignored them, often deliberately avoiding his group. After several days of overt belligerence, I knew that it could no longer be ignored. At the point I felt that I could overlook the animosity no more, I learned through Ghadoh that Veritani had gleaned the truth of my injuries from Nirrox and his friends. It seemed that it was jealousy which had driven Nirrox, he and his friends thought that I, an outsider, was being favoured by the villagers, and recently unwittingly appearing to court the person of his desire – Vilucia.

That evening the tranquillity in the village was disturbed as Veritani called for everyone to congregate in the village centre. Curiously, we gathered as a crowd in the large area in front of the High priest's hut. Veritani stared at me with his hollow eyes and then beckoned Jisa, Grimat, Ghadoh and myself forward.

Gesturing with a flourish of his hand, two elders dragged Nirrox out of Veritani's hut by his hair and threw him in front of the High priest. Veritani slowly stooped down, and grasping Nirrox by his throat, pulled him upright so that the tips of his toes dangled loosely in the dust. Veritani then swept his hand behind his robe and brought out a shiny knife, its keen blade glinting in the afternoon sun. The edge of the blade was then held to Nirrox's throat, nicking his skin to allow the first pools of his life blood to trickle down his neck. Nirrox's friends stood nearby, closely watched by other village elders. Veritani looked at me waiting for me to give some sign. It was the Siculi way that expected me, as the victim of their actions, to determine their punishment. Shocked at what was expected of me I remained stoic.

"Ka'desh, it is your right to mete punishment on these wrongdoers." Veritani boomed, "what is your decision? Do you call death, or do you call dishonour?"

I called upon my Melita upbringing and guidance as I silently beseeched my gods.

"Revered One," I softly spoke, "I cannot find malice enough in my heart to bring such a terrible punishment. If it pleases you and the gods, and your kinfolk here present, I believe that their continued existence in the village would bring eventual contrition."

A gasp rippled through the crowd. This surprised and shocked Veritani and the villagers. This was definitely not the way of the Siculi.

"I suggest that their penalty instead be that of subservience to my benefactors, Jisa and Grimat, for a period of one year." I continued, "this is my way - the Melita way – no retribution nor reprisal, that only through forgiveness and contriteness that true penitence can be attained."

Veritani and the villagers' mouths were opened in shock. It was assumed that death would be the accepted punishment. That this visitor from another land had the temerity to dismiss what had always been the way was unheard of.

Veritani released Nirrox and raised his hands high. Nirrox fell to the ground, then recomposing himself but understandably mystified as to the turn of events, scuttled over to his four friends who were cowering in the background, though still under the watchful eyes of the elders.

"So it must be." Veritani thundered, and then pointing his bony finger at Nirrox and his companions stated, "Nirrox, Bagra, Shira, Pola and Comano - you are now enslaved to Jisa and Grimat for a period of one year. You will be at their call at all times of the day and will do their bidding without complaint nor compromise. Should you fail in your punishment, then you will face my judgement alone. There will be no second chance."

It was fully understood by all the villagers what that judgement would be. Deep inside, the prospect disgusted me, but as an outsider it was not my position to argue further. Veritani's verdict was final.

From that day, my domestic tasks with Grimat and Jisa became fewer, what with Nirrox and his fellow miscreants now undertaking them. I was now getting more involved in village affairs to the extent that I was now privy to much of the daily organisation of the village and its defence against Sicani raiders. Much of this defence was of an overt and protective posture, such as repairing the ditch and embankment which girt the village and crop area, and strengthening the two entrance gates at each end of the enclosure.

These efforts were not in vain. One night while Ra'barak and Xita'klil argued, sending flashes of lightning and torrents of rain upon us, a raiding party of about 20 Sicani attempted to cross the ditch near to where a copse of low trees grew and enter the village. Fortunately, the sentries were vigilant and the alarm was quickly raised. All those menfolk of the village who had been sanctioned by the elders to bear weapons, myself included, rallied to our allotted posts. Ghadoh and I belonged to the defence party, so named because they would immediately go to the location of the incursion and repel the intruders. We were with this group because of our prowess with knife and spear. Veritani stood well back, raising his hands into the air and uttering curses upon the attackers.

This was my first such encounter and my gut trembled in anticipation. Or was it trepidation? My heart told me it was wrong to harm another, but my head was willing to protect my patrons.

In the gloom and occasional flash of lightning we could see the Sicani raiders flitting from shadow to shadow. They were very adept at raiding and used their art skilfully. We were strung out along the embankment – about 30 of us. There were others in the shadows behind us, ready to move up in support should they be needed. The lightning flashed and the erect figure of a man appeared in front of me; reflexes took control. The spear left my hand and penetrated the figure in his stomach. He collapsed silently, perhaps the excitement of the foray along with the thunder and noise of the rain quietened the sounds. Glancing around, I darted forward and retrieved my spear. Another Sicani appeared on my left, who I disembowelled with a slash of my knife, his blood and entrails splattering over me. I was not concerned, I knew that I would probably be covered with another's blood in due course and that the rain, still teeming down, would wash it away. I wiped the water from my eyes and saw to my right Ghadoh and another villager in a violent struggle with several raiders. With no immediate threat to myself at this point, I rushed over to assist, approaching from behind the assailants to slash their backs with my knife, followed by a swift lunge with my spear into their sides.

All too quickly it was over. The morning light was just starting to appear and the rain had stopped. We gathered ourselves together, attending to any who were injured and to ascertain whether any villager had been killed, or worse, taken as a prize for slavery or ransom. We seemed to have been fortunate with no serious injuries and none apparently missing. As for the attackers, they left no casualties behind, although they left a large quantity of their life blood washing away into the earth.

There was a shout behind from within the village. Veritani and another man were approaching hastily.

"We have not been that fortunate after all," Veritani soothed to our group. Then his dark penetrating eyes looked straight into mine, and he continued, "Vilucia has been taken!"

My heart sank, my mouth went dry and my knees trembled.

Veritani spoke again, pointing to several men gathered.

"Ghadoh, you and two others will trail the Sicani and attempt to rescue Vilucia from their filthy clutches. With their slain and wounded, they will find their progress laborious. Do not engage them in battle, they will surely overcome you. But do what you must to bring her back."

I began to protest, saying that I should be going.

Veritani directed at me, "no! Ka'desh. You will not go. Your heart will govern your actions and that will be dangerous for you and your companions."

The trio, led by Ghadoh, filed across the ditch and into the forest from where the Sicani had come.

My mind was in turmoil all day, not knowing whether she was alive or dead. It was late in the afternoon when the trio returned. I fell to my knees in shock and grief. Dragging a rough frame made from tree branches behind them, they emerged from the forest. The lifeless and unmistakable form of Vilucia lay on the frame, her body bruised and beaten, her clothing tattered and torn.

Hands held me back as Ghadoh and the two others forlornly staggered with their load into the centre of the village to Veritani's hut. Veritani emerged and strode over to the body now laid on the ground. With a flourish, he flicked his cape off his shoulders and laid it over Velucia's tortured corpse to cover it from curious eyes.

Ghadoh approached Veritani and in hushed tones whispered into his ear. Veritani fell to his knees and, raising his head skywards, shrieked an unearthly ululation. The whole village followed suit, the noise resounding throughout the hills and mountains. Two elders then furtively approached, and, lifting the bier, took it to the doorway of Velucia's hut where her grief-stricken parents waited. Villagers prepared a platform and gently raised Velucia's body onto it. There, her mother and father would clean and prepare her body for burial in their family tomb. Although the village was united in their grief, this was to be a private occasion.

Heartbroken once again, I went to the beach to sit on the sand and mourn alone. I looked up and pleaded with Bu'sa to release me from this pain. Why have the gods tortured me so, I asked them, by stealing my happiness, preventing me from having a loving relationship with a life partner. Tears of grief flowed down my cheeks and fell like droplets of rain on the sand. My mind wandered aimlessly between sorrow and anger. I became angry with the ancients who had foretold my future, angry with Iskef and Veritani who were upholding the ancients' prophecies, and annoyed that I had followed blindly their direction.

Wiping the tears from my eyes, I abruptly stood and turned on my heels. As I lifted my head, Veritani's form appeared in front of me. Startled, I stopped. He stretched his bony hand out and rested it on my shoulder. The soothing touch of his fingers on my skin allayed my anger.

"Ka'desh, my son," his voice was now soft and comforting, "you are in pain, I can understand that, you have every right to be. But your emotion is misplaced; do not direct your anger at the ancients, it will be wasted effort. The ancients are long gone and only their words have power this day. Instead direct your emotion towards healing, not only yours but that of all whose lives were affected by Velucia. Her memory will always be within you,. it is how you treat that memory which will define your respect of her."

Before I could respond, he removed his hand and wraithlike, disappeared in the shadows. Again, I was in turmoil. His words had resonated deeply within me, but I still had a hatred of those who had despoiled her. It was at that point that my gods, those whom I had grown with, answered me and gave me a sign. A dark cloud had formed hiding Sem'a's glow, and Ra'barak flashed his hand to earth with an almighty crash. I was thrown down onto my face in the sand, momentarily dazed. When I had regained my senses, I found that I was surrounded by a radiance, a radiance emitted from Sem'a's eye through a tiny opening in the cloud. It felt as if tiny barbs were prickling my skin. My hair, normally dark and dense on my head and shoulders, waved in an unmoving wind as the prickles moved over my scalp.

I clutched at the figurine still on its cord around my neck as a voice reverberated in my head, silent to all but me. In a moment I recognised it as my father's voice.

"Ka'desh," it softly spoke, "don't be afraid. Do not harbour ill-will, as it will only infect your mind. Your ancestors are with you, always watching. You are my son and I will always guide you."

All too soon the sensation passed, the clouds were gone and I was left lying on the sand in the warm glow of Sem'a's breath. It was only then that I realised that the ancients had spoken to me through my father, whom I could never disregard. It was now clear that my life was being redefined and redirected by forces beyond my comprehension.

I slowly trudged back to the village, lost in my thoughts and grief. Wiping the tears from my eyes I silently entered our hut and curled up to sleep.

The next day was a contradictory day of mourning and celebration. We mourned the loss of a young life, yet also celebrated the joy which that young life gave us. During the morning Veritani and several elders took Velucia's shrouded body to the temple where, in accordance with the secret traditions of the Siculi, they performed a series of ceremonies and incantations. Upon the completion of these rituals, her body was returned to her family. At around midday, the village gathered around Velucia's family as her father and brother picked up the litter carrying her still form, tightly wrapped in cloth and bound with straps of leather. I had managed to find some locally made dye to mix with some earth to paint my face with blue and white stripes as Iskef had done, at what seemed a lifetime ago. This was my way of honouring Velucia and giving my ancestors permission to accept her as one of their own. As a procession, we walked a short way through the trees to a high, grassy hillock. As we approached, I noticed a huge, rounded stone had been rolled aside to reveal a dark passageway leading deep into the mound. The passageway, I had been told, led to a central space where the recently departed were laid to rest alongside some of their personal belongings, which they could take to the afterlife.. As we congregated near the entrance, Velucia's father and brother slowly walked through the crowd and into the gloomy confines within. Veritani solemnly walked behind until he too disappeared into the gloom. After a short time, amid loud wailing and ululations from the womenfolk, the three re-emerged. Veritani then directed four men to replace the stone in the entrance and the crowd dissipated in groups, back to the village to continue the celebration of Velucia's life.

In the village centre near to the High priest's hut, a large pyre had been prepared and benches set up with every type of fresh food imaginable laid out on them. I was drawn along with the crowd to this place, and as we neared, a cacophony of music began. Couples and groups were drawn in by this and began to whirl and dance in an almost hypnotic, trance-like state. Draughts of a potent elixir were drawn and consumed by almost everyone. After two such drinks, my head began spinning and I could not stop laughing and shouting. I remembered the drink that my father had given me in another lifetime and the similarities were very strong.

Ghadoh grabbed my arm and shepherded me to one side to where Jisa and Grimat stood watching. My head cleared as I stared at them. It was then that I realised how old and frail they both now appeared. I raised my arms to hold them both, but my intoxicated body had other ideas as I stepped forward and fell flat on my face. I felt gentle hands lift me up as my head reeled. I tried to speak but my mouth had would not synchronise with my words.

"Jis….. Rimma," I mumbled, "Wosha doon."

Give up, Ka'desh, my brain told me, I can't even understand you!

My eyes dimmed and everything went blurry. I had a faint sensation of being carried but little else. Then there was a deep darkness.

My eyes strained to open as I heard a voice yelling my name. My head thundered and ached with every breath I took. Slowly the fuzz cleared and I could now see Ghadoh grinning down at me, Jisa and Grimat behind him both also smiling but concerned.

"Your first time?" he asked.

"What?" I muttered as I held my head between my hands.

"You've never had the merry drink before, have you?" He asked again, this time more clearly.

"Aaaaagh!" I groaned, "Is that what it was? Why are there a thousand sheep running around in my head? And why does my mouth taste like the straw from a goat's pen?"

Ghadoh laughed a derisive laugh as he shook his head. Reaching behind him, he picked up a gourd of fresh cold water and went to offer it to me. As soon as I reached up for it, appreciating a long cool drink, he tipped it and its contents over my head, drenching me in refreshingly frigid water.

"That will wake you up." He chuckled as he walked away, "come on, we have things to do."

It was only when my head cleared and I had something to eat that the pain in my head subsided and the horrid taste in my mouth disappeared. It was also then that the memory of Velucia and her passing suddenly haunted me again, and I sat and wept a thousand tears. Jisa came up behind me and placed her soothing hands on my shoulders.

"The pain will pass, my Ka'desh," she consoled, "but it will take time. The memory of her will always be with you."

She lifted her hands and moved away to leave me with my thoughts.

Prisoner

It was later in the season when Sem'a' warmth waned and the skies started to turn dark. The seas churned and the wind howled as Xita'klil and Ra'barak argued. Ghadoh and I braved the wrath of these gods as we walked along the sandy shore, watching the great waves crash upon the beach then suck back out, trying to devour anyone who would venture close. The wind chilled us to the core now that Sem'a no longer warmed her breath. The rain fell gently at first but soon began to drop in torrents. Spotting a cave in the rocks ahead, we made our way to it for shelter.

Water dripped from the roof of the cave as a constant cascade fell over the cave mouth. The sea churned and waves crashed with a roar onto the beach. Attempting to keep dry, we moved further back into the cave. It was then that I realise that this was no ordinary cave - the rock was a glistening black and as hard as flint, the walls rough with sharp edges, threatening to cut our exposed flesh. I was in Xitan's gut and he was ready to digest us as his next meal. I panicked and ran, alarmed at this prospect, out onto the beach. Amongst the deafening roar of the waves and the howling of the intensifying wind I stood, water streaming through my hair and running down my face and body. I looked back at the mouth of the cave and could just discern Ghadoh grinning broadly at me, as I shook like a tree in a summer breeze. Hesitantly, I rejoined him in the cave as the rain teemed down.

"I have been wanting to ask you for a long time," Ghadoh asked me quietly, "but what is the figurine which you wear about your neck?"

"It is Bu'sa, our earth goddess, protector of families," I replied, "this was given to me by my High priest just before I left my village so that I would never forget them."

"You will never forget," Ghadoh responded, "you never forget."

As we squatted in the cave, to change the subject, I endeavoured to explain to him about our gods and why I was so afraid. He nodded his head seemingly knowingly as I explained, but deep inside I felt that he was being kind and simply did not quite understand. I could only hope, that with time, our understanding of each other would become easier to comprehend.

Just as darkness was falling, the rain eased and we made our way back to the village, Ghadoh's hut and some warm food.

Overnight the storm abated somewhat, and we were greeted by Sem'a peering at us rather forlornly through scattered clouds. After eating our morning supper, we gathered in the village centre to be given our daily chores.

Ghadoh and I were given the task of gathering rocks to repair the walls of some of the huts which were damaged during the previous day's rainfall. We picked up two large bags each and headed down the path to the beach to gather suitable rocks. Soon we were on the beach walking towards the rocky outcrop where we sheltered last evening.

"Choose the smooth rocks," Ghadoh advised, "as they are easier to work than the black ones. Those are from Mongibello's mouth and are as hard as flint and cannot be worked easily."

I walked along the beach towards a shoal of suitable stones just on the water's edge. I squatted down and started loading my bag with several large ones.

Suddenly, the ground shook violently in an enormous spasm, sending me tumbling into the encroaching surf. The sky went black amid flashes of light from Ra'barak's fingers, and a thick cloud of noxious, choking, gas billowed down from the side of the mountain in the direction of the village.

"We must go!" Ghadoh yelled frantically, dragging me back to my feet. As we turned to dash away, another tremor shook the earth violently sending us both spiralling into the maddening waters of the ocean. Gasping for breath amongst the spume and spray of the water, and fearful of the erupting Mongibello, we dispensed with our bags which were weighing us down and attempted to hold each other's head up out of the water, as we battled against the tidal currents and the vicious wind. A huge wave swept by, picking us up and carrying us with it. A sodden log brushed beside us bobbing in the swirling waters and we frantically grabbed for it. Holding on for our lives, we rode out the tempest. Unable to sleep, we clung to the log for what seemed an eternity.

When the first vestiges of dawn appeared, we looked around us to find that we were no longer near land. As we could now see that our log was big enough, we wearily climbed up and sat astride it. The storm churned up by Mongibello had long gone but the detritus of its aftermath still lingered in the water around us. Pieces of trees, bits of timber, the shattered prow of a raft and the bodies of animals – a goat, a lamb and a dog – floated nearby. The sun beat mercilessly upon us as the day wore on. Our mouths were dry, our tongues swollen from the saltiness of the water and our bodies wracked with pain and bruises. We looked at the sky and prayed to our respective gods for forgiveness for whatever sins we may have committed.

Bu'sa must have heard us. I heard a shout. We despairingly looked up and an apparition appeared to us. A golden craft with silver wings floated not far from us, a spirit leaning over the side ready to catch us and bring us onto the vessel. In our delirium, we only sensed the strong hands lifting us up and placing us into the safety of the craft. We collapsed exhausted onto the deck, not knowing nor caring whether we were safe or not. When we awoke, we found that it was the latter.

As the weariness left our bodies and we returned to the land of the living, I felt restraints on my legs and wrists. It then dawned on both of us that we were manacled, with thongs of leather around our wrists and ankles, thick rope woven between the thongs so that we could not rise to stand. We could move, but barely. Our limbs, already raw from our recent excursion, were made more so by the course leather affixed around our arms and legs. My heart sank.

Bu'sa, I asked, what have we done?

One of the boat people came over to us and offered a bladder of water. We both eagerly drank, feeling the freshness of the cool water dissolve the bitter saltiness from our mouths. The person went away but soon returned offering us hard scraps of bread, which we also ravenously ate. Not a word was exchanged. Fatigued, I looked around me to take in these new surroundings. I curiously noticed a pile of white cloth at the other end of the vessel, with the vague outline of a young woman beneath it, but thought nothing more of it. After a short while, the motion of the craft churning in the sea lulled us both again to sleep.

The sleep was short-lived. We abruptly awoke to the craft tossing about violently, waves crashing over its sides, the crew frantically trying to steer it to safety. The vessel sheered around and a wave crashed over it nearly washing us overboard. The wind shrieked and whistled deafeningly around us. Ghadoh spotted a knife sliding about the floor of the vessel and frantically grabbed at it. Sawing at the ropes binding his hands and feet he eventually freed himself, then did the same to me. Another wave crashed down on us. We looked around the vessel and could not see any of our captors.

"They must have been knocked into the sea!" Ghadoh shouted to me through the noise. We fearfully stared at the churning waters, watching waves break menacingly over a nearby reef. Another wave hit the side of the vessel driving it onto the needle-sharp shoal, unceremoniously throwing us into the angry sea. I opened my eyes and all I could see was a mass of broken timbers and ropes around me. I felt myself being pulled down by a coil of rope wrapped around my shin, but still attached to the sinking craft. Panicking, I kicked and tried screaming but all in vain. Then I felt Ghadoh's hands release the tension on my ankle and I looked down to see him slowly sink out of sight into the murky depths.

Freed from the bonds, my body floated upwards, and gasping for breath, I broke through the surface into the frenzy of the storm. I hugged a large piece of timber tossing nearby, and my mind was in confusion as I contemplated my situation. Something in the far reaches of my memory told me that I had seen this before, but weariness overtook the thoughts.

As I floated there clinging to my timber, I felt something soft touch my back. I turned around to discover the body of a young woman floating behind me, her smooth chiselled features glowing in the light and her long blond hair moving unrestrained in the water. I pulled her up to me and then I saw in shock that I knew this woman. She was the one love I had had when younger. It was Nee'sa! My heart stopped beating for a moment and a lump rose in my throat.

No! I cried to myself. No! You cannot be with your ancestors?

I choked back my tears and held her head, kissing her gently on the forehead. Without warning, she opened her eyes and coughed salty water from her throat in a fit of choking spasms. I lifted her head higher out of the water and attempted to get her to hold onto the piece of timber. She looked at me deliriously for a moment, and realising her current predicament, clung desperately to the timber. Then recognition lit up her eyes.

"Ka'desh?" She asked weakly.

I slid my arm around her slim waist to prevent her slipping back into the water.

"Yes, Nee'sa. It is me, Ka'desh," I replied almost apologetically. "Just keep holding onto the timber and we should be safe."

It was not long before I could hear waves crashing on a beach and knew we were very near land. I felt the gritty sensation of sand between my toes as I endeavoured to gain a foothold and bring us both to shore. As we crawled out of the waves, we both fell exhausted onto the sand and fell into a deep sleep.

It was twilight when we awoke, and not knowing what to expect, we walked up the beach to an outcrop of rocks where I found some old dried seaweed to make a soft place to lay for the night. The strange sounds of the night creatures, the soft stirring of the trees in the breeze and the mesmerising sound of the surf, not to mention sheer exhaustion, soon lulled us back into a sleep, but one now tormented by thirst and hunger.

Sem'a shone her radiant warmth on our bodies as we awoke to a new day. We investigated our surroundings carefully. We were not yet sure what kind of wild creatures may be in the trees overlooking the coast in this strange land, and so were apprehensive at venturing inland. In the distance, along the beach, we a thin strand of smoke which indicated the possibility of a village. Lack of food and dehydration drove us toward the smoke.

As we walked along the water's edge, the cool clear sea water swirling around our feet creating eddies of sand in our footprints, we talked. Nee'sa spoke through near tears as she related how I had mysteriously been taken away from Ta'Shema village with no-one speaking of where I had gone. There were many rumours; some said that I had displeased the gods with my choice of not taking a life partner while others said that the priests had me removed as I was a threat to their future. There were many that thought that I had been abducted by cruel traders needing me to crew one of their watercraft.

I told her what had really happened, with no omissions. I told her about the prophecy as told to me by Iskef, and that it was foretold in the Siculi lore. I told her of my dreams and that they made no sense to me. I told her about Ghadoh and his teachings, how Grimat and Jisa took me in as one of their own, and I told her about Velucia. I related the torment I suffered under Nirrox and the anguish I felt with having to direct their punishment. Through my tears I told her of Velucia's death at the hands of the Sicani when they sent the raiding party. Finally, I told her how Ghadoh and I had been swept into the ocean and how Ghadoh, in his final act, saved me from death. Throughout all, Nee'sa listened without interrupting.

"And how did it come to pass that you are here?" I finally asked her.

She told me that after I had disappeared, several months had passed when a trader boat arrived at Cor'din, but had to wait for better weather and winds to make the return voyage. She crept onto the vessel and had hidden herself among a quantity of cloth bundles to follow where I had gone. But when the vessel was near to the Sicani on the side of the island which Bu'sa rests, she was discovered. Her fair skin and blond hair frightened the seafarers who though that she was one of the Fates of the Waters who devoured unsuspecting seafarers, and so she was thrown into the ocean to suffer her own watery fate. By more good fortune than good management, she managed to float ashore by using her saturated dress as an inflated oilskin to which she clung. Washed up onto the beach, she lay exhausted and soon fell asleep. Eventually, she awoke in a small dark cave with the only entrance blocked by a strong gate of stout timber. Again, her complexion angered and terrified the villagers who had pulled her from the seawater. After some time in captivity,-she was not sure how long as she was almost always in the darkness of the cave- she was dragged out to be taken away on the very vessel on which I was eventually taken captive.

I was full of questions, as it had been nearly a year since I had left our home. However, they needed to wait for the meantime, as we were entering the village.

The village stood on a slight rise and was surrounded by a high wooden wall with a gate entryway at each side of the village. The rise afforded the village a certain overview of the surrounding land which mainly consisted of cultivated stands of grain growing in neat rows, and of lines of fresh vegetables sprouting their leafy tops through the freshly turned earth. We could make out rectangular shaped huts within, with high sloping thatched roofs. People were milling around inside but hastily stopped and stared at us as we approached. We made our way through the massive wooden gateway, and the very thought of what such an entrance may be protecting the village from concerned us greatly. Soon, people were drifting around behind us, blocking any potential escape path and propelling us towards the central area of the village. The crowd drew closer to us and their irritation seemed to grow more intense. We stopped and looked around us, bewildered. Suddenly, we were both driven to the ground by a sharp and severe blow to our backs. Before we could gather our wits, we were trussed together with leather thongs and dragged to a half-submerged hut on the very fringe of the village. There, we were thrown into its semi-darkness and the thick wooden door slammed shut and barred on the outside.

Confused and sore, we sat in the gloom gathering in our surroundings. The hut had a circular solid earthen wall which was topped by thick wooden beams leading to the top of a short single pole in the middle of the hut. The roof was thickly thatched to match the others in the village. Off to one side was a pile of skins thrown in disarray on the hard dirt floor. There was a strong smell of stale human bodies and human waste lingering in the air. We quickly discovered that our bonds were not as tight as previously thought and we soon untied them. As we sat rubbing our wrists and ankles, we just stared in amazement at our predicament. We were stunned that we were both now in captivity and amazed that after all this time apart, we had found each other again. We fell against each other, clinging to the present situation and to past memories. Before long, we parted our bodies and lay down together as comfortably as we could on the discarded skins. Completely exhausted, we fell into a deep sleep, thankful to the gods that we were at least still alive.

After seemingly hours had elapsed, the door was flung open, blinding us with the sudden glare of daylight entering our prison. A dark shadow entered the doorway, momentarily blocking the light. Two plain wooden dishes were pushed across the dirt floor towards us. Not a word was spoken. In the dishes we found a grimy, gritty paste which almost passed as being edible. The taste we ignored as our appetites were partially whetted.

The door opened again and what seemed to be the same shadow pushed an earthenware jug into the gloom. Nee'sa reached for it, nearly spilling its contents in her enthusiasm, and greedily drank some of its contents. It was water, a little muddy but still palatable. She offered the jug to me from which I drank as well.

I stood up trying to stretch my aching limbs, and found that I could only stoop owing to the low roof. I picked at the thatch trying to make a hole with through which to peer, but found it was too thick and densely woven, so I crouched over to the door to see if any cracks could be used to discover the outside world. There was one very slight crack where, with a lot of concentration, I could make out several huts and one of the two gates to the village. What surprised me was that the gate had been closed and barred. Was this because of us, I wondered?

It was what seemed to be several days later that there appeared to be a change in the villagers' attitudes. The door was flung open and the figure beckoned for us both to exit. We staggered out into the bright sunlight, squinting at our surroundings. A rough hand pushed us in our backs and we fell to our knees. As we looked up, we saw the gruesome sight of a gnarled and twisted figure of a man. He had the tattered remnants of a loincloth about his waist and several necklaces made up of grizzled and rotting teeth. His face was badly disfigured – a series of deep scars ran down the right side of his face from brow to jaw, his right eye just an empty socket. His lips were painted black with his green teeth sharpened to fine points. His hair was just a tuft at the back tied into some sort of tail, the remainder of his head a convolution of deep scarring. The hair at the back of my scalp tingled at the sound of Nee'sa as she shrieked at the sight of him.

He spoke through that horrible orifice in the tongue I had learned with the Siculi.

"What manner of creature are you?" He screamed hysterically, "you come to us from the ocean with your fine white skins."

He snatched at Nee'sa's blond hair and roughly pulled her up.

"You are the Sykex, the spawn of the creatures of the deep. Your skin has not seen the warmth of day so it betrays you as one," he screamed, and then raising his voice higher, "WE WILL NOT LET YOU BRING MISFORTUNE ON OUR PEOPLE!"

He dropped Nee'sa back to her knees, then his long scrawny fingers gripped around my throat and wrenched me up.

"You will die to save our people." He hissed. "You will die by the fire which will devour your watery bodies and you will disappear into the air of the mountains as a wisp of vapour."

I was dropped back to the ground. Unseen hands then grabbed us both by the hair and we were dragged back into our prison and the door slammed shut once more.

Once I knew that we were alone, I turned to Nee'sa.

"We must get out of here," I said softly to her.

"But how?" she asked, "the door is bolted and the roof is too thick. It would take too long to make a hole for us to escape."

I went to the back side of the hut and clawed at the earth; it was relatively soft.

"I think that I may be able to dig under the wall here." I whispered encouragingly. I noticed that our food bowls had not been taken away, so soon we used them to quietly dig away at the earth under the wall. As we dug away, the earth we were removing we scattered around the floor next to the wall of the hut. It was not too long before I could force my arm through a small hole to the outside of the hut. As it was now dark and we could no longer see clearly where we were digging, we decided to stop and resume the following day. Reluctantly we snuggled into the warm skins and fell asleep.

It had been daylight for some time before anyone came to our hut. The door was brusquely thrown open and two burly figures entered and crudely dragged us by the arms outside. The horrible creature we had encountered the previous day was there to greet us. Rough hands pushed us to our knees in front of the creature.

Its grizzled face with its fetid breath scowled down at us.

"Your time is coming nearer, my little treasures," it hissed derisively, "and as a warning to all of your kind, you will build your own funeral pyre."

It giggled hysterically and then added to several of the villagers, "show them where they will end their days!"

A kick and a shove in our backs and we were back on our feet, being manhandled to a pile of brushwood and timber. Beside the pile were two tall poles already blackened by fire, the ashes from those fires still laying around each pole. No further instruction was needed, we were both fully conversant with what was required.

For the remainder of the day we piled brushwood and logs around the poles until the pile was at head height. Only then were we led back to the hut which was our prison.

Once our door was secured, we again began digging with some urgency until a small hole appeared under the wall into the daylight outside. I managed to get my head into the hole and took a look. The main defensive wall was only a step or two away and the main gate which had been barred a few days earlier was now open. We expanded the hole as large as we dared and hid our handiwork with the hides. We decided that we would wait until later that night before risking an escape. It would offer us our best chance at not being seen.

We had just rearranged the skins to look as normal as possible when the door was flung open and the meagre scraps of food and dirty water were dropped unceremoniously into our bowls again. We did not eat, instead we preserved what food we could carry and waited patiently for night to descend.

It seemed like an eternity passed before we felt it was right to go. Carefully listening for any disturbances, we moved the skins from the hole and silently crawled through to the defensive wall of the village. At this stage we could not see any sentries. Moving along the shadows of the wall, we crept our way to the gate, stopping in the shadow of one of the large supporting pylons. There were two sentries, but they seemed to be more interested in an animal prowling nearby. Taking full advantage of this, we stealthily slipped past them and into the trees. Without a sound, we made our way through the undergrowth until we came to an outcrop of rocks overlooking the seashore and the village enclosure. Thus far our presence had not been missed. The village was still quiet and the sentries on the gate we had so recently slipped through were oblivious to our departure.

The night was dark. Ka'mah- our people's moon god- was sleeping. In hushed voices, Nee'sa and I discussed our next move. We both agreed that we would need to get as far from the village as possible before it was discovered we had escaped. Leaving caution to the wind, we bravely walked to the seashore.

Adhering as closely as possible to the rough scrub and tall grasses growing on the low dunes, we hurriedly ran. It was only after some time I realised that we were going in the opposite direction to which we had originally arrived. Maybe it was the gods smiling at us that we had made that choice. After all, that creature in the village would probably come to the conclusion that we would go back from whence we had come and therefore retrace our steps.

Running through the loose sand of the dunes was in one way a blessing, as the sand quickly fell back into the holes our feet made as we ran to hide our steps, but in another it was a disadvantage as it made the running so much harder. Before long we were both exhausted and stopped to catch our breath. We quickly realised that we were very exposed in the whiteness of the sand so we moved into the undergrowth, carefully listening for any sound which would have indicated our escape. Several minutes passed before we continued, this time at a casual pace but still very conscious of any noises around us. All we heard were the distant baying and barking of dogs, the occasional howl of a jackal and the breeze in the trees.

We continued along the seashore, mainly because in the dimness of the night we could make out the sand, and the splashing of the water disguised any sound we may have made. Soon the vestiges of dawn began, with Se'ma's glow slowly rising over the distant hills and mountains. Fearful that we would be seen in the approaching light, we pushed our way through the scrub and grass and up a high rocky knoll which gave us a clear view all around and hid us from any searching eyes. Grateful for our newfound sanctuary, we collapsed together and soon fell asleep in the coarse grass growing among the rocks.

It seemed an age we had lain there asleep when a loud noise woke us both with a start. I peered cautiously over the rocks and froze. I was looking straight into the face of a wild pig, a huge boar, its razor-sharp fangs dripping with saliva as it snorted and pawed the ground. Nee'sa started rising beside me but I gestured for her to remain still. The pig and I continued our staring game, neither of us moving, each watching the other intently waiting for a sudden move. I very nearly flinched as Nee'sa clutched my leg, fear trembling through her body. I remained unmoving with my eyes fixed on the boar, remembering the lesson Ghadoh had taught me what seemed a lifetime ago. As then, the boar lost interest and wandered back down the knoll. It was at that moment that I recognized that, despite everything I had been taught as a child about harming others whether they be creatures or man, we would need some form of protection in this strange new land we were traversing, as I had needed when with the Siculi.

I raised my eyes to the heavens beseeching the gods as to the meaning of my quest. I received only silence, I thought that the gods had abandoned me. Nee'sa stared into my eyes, not understanding my quandary. I wished to ignore all the emotion which had surrounded my life; take Nee'sa as my life partner and settle somewhere here in this new land, but the words of Iskef echoed deeply in my mind.

Hunger grumbled in our stomachs. We unwrapped the meagre provisions we had salvaged at the village and greedily ate. It would still be several hours before it would be dark and we could continue our escape. Looking around, I took in our environs. Back the way we had fled I could see the wisps of smoke from the village. Ahead of us lay more forest for a short way before rolling into a grassy knoll, the crest of which housed another walled village just discernible in the haze. It was there that I wanted to go, if only to procure food if possible. Our previous experience made us very wary of approaching blindly, and in the meantime we needed water as we were both very parched. Looking around again, I saw what appeared to be a stream a short distance inland and on the way to the newly spotted village.

Once dusk had set in and the evening shadows had disappeared, we crept from our hideaway towards the forest. We soon came upon a well-worn path leading towards the stream, and having little other alternative, very cautiously followed it. Ever conscious of any strange noises, we scooped water in our hands to drink. Without any interruptions, we had our fill and silently continued down the path.

After some time, the closeness of the trees thinned and made way to an undulating plain with the lights of campfires in a village visible in the distance. Fearing that our shadows cast by Ka'mah would betray us, we stayed near to the tree line, skirting close to the village.

This village was very similar to the one where we were imprisoned, with a stout wall of vertical timbers surrounding it and a guarded entrance at each end. Fortunately, the sentries were not very vigilant and so did not see us creeping past the walled enclosure. Hurriedly, we found the path again and briskly but soundlessly put some distance between us and the village before Sem'a returned to light up the day.

Just as the first rays of Sem'a's light began creeping over the distant hills, we left the path, making our way through the trees to a low rise where we could observe our surroundings as we bided our time before night once more. As we lay on the carpet of grasses on the knoll, I became acutely aware of the rumblings of hunger stirring in my stomach. Nee'sa heard the noise as well and then stifled a giggle as her own stomach growled.

"We need food," I said, stating the obvious. Nee'sa stared at me, as if expecting me to immediately come up with an answer.

"If I had a spear, I could hunt for something," I absently said, then recoiled at the memory of the events at the Siculi village. Feeling a twinge of remorse at the lives which had been lost, I was immediately confronted with the recollection of Velucia and her brutal demise. I cringed at the thought which only made me want to hold Nee'sa close. I had lost one love, I did not want to lose another.

"Let us continue walking until we find another village," Nee'sa reasoned. "Maybe they will treat us better than the other village did and give us some food."

"It's a risk," I replied, "but we need to eat else we will perish."

With that, we tacitly decided that we would stop at the next village and beg for food. With that plan in store, we curled up in each other's arms for warmth and dozed until evening.

As the evening shadows fell, we left our little sanctuary and returned to the path. In the cool night air and under Ka'mah's glow, we quickly strolled. There were times when the trees hid Ka'mah from us and we found ourselves fighting our way through branches, giggling and laughing. Very quickly though, we realised that our safety depended upon our silence.

After some time hiking in near darkness, fumbling our way along the path, we saw in the distance the flickering lights from fires. Warily, we crept along the path towards the light, always keeping the cover of the trees very near. Presently, we came into a small clearing with a village set some distance back from the path. It too was surrounded by a high wall of timber logs, but unlike the others we had seen there were no sentries posted at the gate. In fact there was no gate, only a large gap in the wall. Following the shadows, we slipped through the gap and furtively looked around. At the centre of the village a huge bonfire was burning, a large group of people seated around it gaily talking and drinking. I made my way to the first hut before us and cautiously crawled around the wall to the doorway of the hut. Fortunately, our eyes had become accustomed to the darkness and so we could see that the hut was empty. I spotted a woven basket with several loaves of coarse wheaten bread and a jug of water very near the doorway. I signalled to Nee'sa, pointing to the food. Her face broke into a grin as we both eagerly grabbed two loaves and the jug. As we crept back outside, we were startled by a young man who appeared from the side of the hut, apparently having just relieved himself against the timber wall.

"Hey," he yelled in the language of the Sicani, "what are you doing?"

Like startled lambs, we ran out through the gate and across the clearing to the path. The youth had rallied several other villagers and they made chase. We ran and ran, we felt our lives depended on it. Flashes of excruciating pain shot through my chest as I struggled to keep my breath. Nee'sa's thin frame streaked ahead of me and I found another fresh burst of energy. The path meandered around large trees and clumps of shrubbery and we followed it as hastily as we could. We could hear the crashing of the villagers pursuing us close by.

The path twisted sharply around a large boulder and as we dashed around, we felt hands grab our arms, twisting us off the trail. Then we both felt hands covering our mouths to stifle any noise. My chest was heaving and I found it difficult to breathe. I could barely see Nee'sa in the gloom but could sense that she was the same. The villagers ran noisily past us, their racket slowly abating in the distance.

The hands on our arms and mouths relaxed and gestured for us to follow them along an obscure pathway scarcely visible in the undergrowth. We followed closely, still clutching our ill-gotten wares. After what seemed an age, we climbed a rocky hill and squeezed through a narrow slit in the rocks to enter a large, dry cave. The hands gestured again to follow and we were led in the inky blackness along a tight passageway until we detected the flickering light of torches burning in a cavern deep within the hillside. It was then we saw our rescuers.

A man who appeared to be not that much older than myself and a woman of the same age. Both were dressed in animal skins

– a vest covering their chests with another sewn from pieces to form a loincloth. Their bodies were filthy with grime, their hair matted with mud, their feet bare on the sandy floor. As we became accustomed to the light, we saw their faces for the first time. His face was gnarled, not with age but with the experience and wisdom of living on ones wits. His eyes were a vivid blue which matched to a certain extent the colour of his teeth, which were mostly broken and sharp. The woman was an enigma. She had the physical qualities of a once attractive woman, but again circumstance had hardened her features to match those of her partner.

The man gestured to the food we held. Nee'sa pulled it back and held it behind her. He emitted a low, nasty growl like a wolf and barked. Nee'sa drew back in fear. The woman moved between Nee'sa and the man, turning to him and growling the same type of growl.

Then, surprisingly, she turned to Nee'sa and spoke in Meliti, our native tongue.

"I am sorry for my friend. He has forgotten his manners living here."

Flabbergasted, Nee'sa and I looked at each other.

"May all of our gods be praised," I squeaked in surprise.

"None of your gods will help you here in this ungodly land!" The man spoke in Meliti. "Here they are nothing but stupid brutes and animals."

"Again, please forgive my friend," the woman continued, "we have not been treated very well by the people of this land and that is why we must live like this, in hiding, eking our existence from stolen food. My name is Mar'sa and my companion is Shon'tel."

"Ka'desh and Nee'sa," I replied, pointing in turn to myself then Nee'sa.

"How do you know the language of the Meliti?" I asked.

"Bah!" Shon'tel shrugged, "It's too long a story to tell. And it's not one I care to share."

"We came with traders many years ago seeking a new life." Mar'sa continued. "As I have already intimated, we were not well treated. We managed to escape from the village and have lived here since. When we lived in Melita, we lived in a village near to Hajarim. It is now impossible for us to return as we have nothing to trade in return for safe passage, either across this accursed land, nor to the Siculi, nor to the water journey home."

She stood staring at us for a moment, then shaking her head, she looked forlornly at the ground. Shon'tel put his hands on her shoulders, and she slowly looked up to see Nee'sa offering her bread to her. I then did the same. Mar'sa looked up at each of us in turn and gently took the bread offered.

"Come," she ordered, "we eat now."

We squatted on some skins on the dusky floor of the cavern, observing our new-found hosts in the wavering light of the torches. We devoured our bread in silence, occasionally dipping it into a shallow dish of olive oil Mar'sa had placed between us on the skins. The ensuing silence interspersed by the infrequent brush of feet became almost deafening.

Nee'sa spoke, interrupting the silence.

"Are all the villages here unwelcoming to strangers?" She asked.

"Only those near the ocean," replied Shon'tel mumbling through mouthfuls of food. "If you have the fair skin such as you, they think that you are an evil spirit sent by their sea god to gather slaves. The only way to kill these spirits is by burning them so that their watery bodies will dissolve into the air."

"I have heard that the villages much further north are more accepting," Mar'sa continued, "they see many more people not of their race and are ready for changes, which would make their hard existence easier."

Shon'tel stopped chewing and became pensive for a moment then glowered at us.

"You may stay as our guests for two days then you must leave. Those villagers will still be looking for you. That they cannot find you will only confirm to them that you are evil spirits and have used your powers to disappear. This only makes it more dangerous for you to remain here. We have remained hidden in this labyrinth of caves for a long time, but it is only a matter of time before one of those villagers will gather his courage and explore. I do not want your existence here to be the reason for such courage."

I looked at Nee'sa and her at me. It was only then I realised how bedraggled we must both appear. Our clothes were in tatters and covered in filth. Nee'sa's once pure white dress was hanging in strips of decaying cloth, her long blond hair a tangle of matted knots, her face and legs covered in a veneer of dirt. I could only imagine what I must look like. As if she had known what was in our heads, Mar'sa hustled off to a corner of the cave to rummage through a pile of skins and cloth. Proudly standing up, she flicked with a flourish a mass of pale blue cloth into Nee'sa's hands. Nee'sa held the cloth up to her body and the familiar shape of a flowing robe revealed itself. Mar'sa bustled Nee'sa to a far corner of the cave where she was hidden from we men's sight.

After some time, the women returned. Nee'sa had washed herself and she now glowed with the freshness of her white skin. The robe clung to her thin proportions, the lower part billowing like a sail around her legs. She was a vision of beauty and I found that I could only stare at her.

"See what we can turn up?" Mar'sa exuberantly bubbled. "Now let us see if those village ingrates would burn such a beautiful thing."

I still stared. Shon'tel gruffly grunted his approval and continued picking at crumbs on the mats.

"Is there...." I stammered embarrassingly, "is there anywhere I could wash?"

Shon'tel looked up then begrudgingly arose.

"Come." He ordered, and I followed meekly. We walked to the back of the cave near to where Nee'sa and Mar'sa had gone but turned down another passageway. Shon'tel had lit a torch as we went past it, and by its dim light we found our way deeper into the hillside.

"Stop!" Shon'tel warned abruptly. I froze. Shon'tel brought the lamp around then crouched on his knees. There in front of him was nothing but blackness. Shon'tel picked up a pebble and flicked it into the void. After several moments I heard a splash as the pebble found the water at the bottom.

"This is where we get our fresh water from," Shon'tel explained, "it is as pure as the snows in winter and tastes just as good."

It was then I saw a bucket tied to a rope which Shon'tel grabbed, tossing the bucket into the depths below, then raising it.

When he placed the full bucket on the ground, he said one word.

"Taste!"

And I did, cupping my hands in the water and lifting it to my lips. It was as pure as the snow and just as cold, and it was immensely refreshing.

"Wash!" Shon'tel directed. I did as I was bidden, washing and rinsing the grime from my body. Soon I felt that I could not clean another spot and gestured to the now soiled water in the bucket.

Shon'tel picked it up and strode back up the passage some distance, me obediently following with the torch. He ducked into a side alcove and emptied the contents of the bucket into a depression. He looked at my enquiring face.

"The water will drain through the ground leaving all the grime and unpleasantness to the earth. It then returns from whence it came for us to use again."

It all made clear sense to me as we placed the bucket at the abyss and then returned to the main cave to re-join Nee'sa and Mar'sa. The women had pulled out a number of thick, plush skins and made beds for us all. It felt now as if it was very late (it was difficult to judge the time of day in the dark of the cave), weariness was overtaking us. We snuggled into our respective beds and fell into a deep sleep.

I had another dream. I dreamt that I was walking along a path towards a village. Nee'sa was not with me, and an immense sadness was over me. What the sadness was I could not identify, but I had this terrible sense that something had happened to Nee'sa, which was why she wasn't with me. I awoke with a start, perspiration dripping from my body. As my eyes adjusted to my surroundings, I realised that it was just another dream. I closed my eyes, but I was unable to immediately resume sleep as the foreboding remained teasing my mind.

It seemed an eternity since I had closed my eyes, but I was suddenly aroused by Mar'sa shaking my arm.

"Wake up!" She cried frantically, "You must leave now!"

Wiping my eyes with my hands I slowly arose in the gloom of the cave. Nee'sa was already awake. There was no sign of Shon'tel.

"Quickly," Mar'sa frantically rushed us, "you must go! The villagers are looking for you and know you are hiding in these caves. There are many ways in and it is only a matter of time before they find one."

Hurriedly, we packed a few items of food and a skin of water into a coarse cloth bag and were bustled through another passage of the cave into daylight. As we stood in a grove of trees outside the narrow, almost hidden entrance, we realised that this was a different way to that which we had entered. A light rain was falling and a thin mist was descending upon us.

"Where is Shon'tel?" Nee'sa asked.

"He is trying to confuse the villagers. He is leading them around the other side of the mountain into caves which will lead nowhere. It will give you time to get away." Mar'sa replied and then warned, "but be very careful on this side of the mountain. The paths can be very treacherous and the cliffs are very steep. Keep away from the ocean and keep going inland. Keep the sun on your right in the mornings and go towards the mountains. The villagers there will help you."

Hurriedly we bid our goodbyes as I gingerly pushed through the undergrowth, gripping Nee'sa' hand. We stumbled onto a narrow pathway and ran along it through the heavy scrub. Thin branches whipped at our faces and legs as we fled. After a while, in order to catch our breath, we stopped and crawled into the trees out of sight. We listened carefully but could not hear any sign of pursuit. We continued along the path which wound its way up and around the hilly slopes. The trees suddenly thinned and soon we were picking our way along the path around great boulders to the crest of the mountain. Suddenly I stopped, Nee'sa stumbling up against me.

"Why did you stop?" She asked.

"Look!" I explained as we peered past over a rocky outcrop. A yawning abyss opened in front of me, a sheer cliff dropping precipitously to a wooded ravine way below. A narrow ledge crept along the cliff face down towards the bottom of the ravine.

"Follow me." I cautioned, "keep as close to the cliff as you can. Do not look down, only where you are putting your feet."

Carefully we made our way down the path, hugging the rock face as we went. Every now and then we would accidentally kick or dislodge a small rock and it would clatter noisily down the cliff sending shivers down my back. I felt something softly hitting my head and I looked up. We were about halfway down the cliff. A dozen heads appeared over the top of the cliff, disturbing the dirt causing it to fall on my head. Then a dozen voices began shouting at us. Abruptly, the shouting ceased and then more dust and pebbles began falling around us. Looking up again we saw the figures pushing a huge boulder to the edge of the cliff. At first panic set in but quickly settled. Nee'sa screamed as she saw the boulder topple over the edge.

"Lean against the cliff," I shouted to her, "as hard as you can."

With our faces hard against the rock, we could feel the vibrations of the boulder as it bounced its way towards us. It crashed its way over the narrow ledge on which we were standing, creating a small avalanche of dirt and rock, which destroyed the part of the ledge which we had just passed. As soon as that danger was over, we moved off, picking our way down the path. The villagers above had located another boulder and pushed it over the ledge. They were learning fast – this time they had selected a spot in front of us. The boulder collided with the path, obliterating the way ahead. We stopped to gather our thoughts. I looked at the scant remains of the path ahead.

"We can do this." I confidently said to Nee'sa, "just tread where I tread. We will be safe."

Nee'sa nervously nodded her head and gingerly followed me. There was only a small section of the path destroyed, and I determined that with two or three steps, we should be able to pass over the damage. I selected a rock still jutting out of the cliff as my first stepping point. As I put my weight on the rock, it broke to tumble away, very nearly with me as well. I heard Nee'sa sigh with relief as I regained my footing. I tried another rock and this time it held. Keeping my momentum up I swung with my feet across the gap and managed to stop on the other side.

"Come on, Nee'sa. You can do it. Just do what I did." I encouraged.

She stretched her leg and placed her foot on the rock. Gripping the stony cliff face, she swung herself across to the midway point then stepped wide to the ledge where I was ready to grab her. As she swung across, I reached over and seized her arm, steadying her and assisting her to the ledge.

She moved towards me and stepped onto the ledge. I breathed a sigh of relief as she started to fall into my open arms.

Unexpectedly, she screamed as her foot slipped off the ledge and she stumbled against me. My heart pounded as we momentarily paused to regain our senses. Looking up for our antagonists, it appeared that they had given up their pursuit of us as they were nowhere to be seen. Comforted by this knowledge, we moved a little faster down the ledge toward the bottom.

Once at the safety of the base of the cliff, we ducked around boulders and shoulders in order to remain relatively hidden from any eyes above. After a short distance, we were surrounded by low shrubbery which afforded us some security. Our bodies were being drained of any further ability to run as we crashed our way through the undergrowth. Soon, totally exhausted, we stopped in a small clearing, shaded by a few larger and leafier trees. Collapsing into each other's arms, we lay on the ground trying to regain the strength to carry on.

The first rays of Bu'sa's light were falling around us when I eventually arose and awoke Nee'sa. I quickly looked around us, suddenly realising how exposed and defenceless we were. Gathering the few items which we had, we made our way into the trees. I knew that we needed a sanctuary in which to hide until nightfall when it would be safer to move on. We found a thicket of scrub which suited our needs, and oblivious to the scraping and scratching of the sharp branches, we crawled into the centre of the thicket. A carpet of rotting leaves and bark lay on the ground to form a natural bed, where we spread our weary forms and soon fell asleep.

Adventure

I awoke to something grunting and snorting heavily into my face. My eyes flickered open, my senses dimmed and for an instant not aware where I was. I had been dreaming that I was in my own bed in my family's hut in Ta'Shema, my brother blowing into my face and calling me. My eyes cleared. I lifted my head. I was unsure as to who was the most startled – me, Nee'sa or the cute little furry creature sniffing my face. It jumped off me and warily stared at me as I slowly raised myself up. As hungry as I was, I knew that I could not kill this creature. Besides, it was just as scared as I was. I held my hand out to it as I would to a strange goat in my own country. The creature crept forward, sniffed my extended fingers and then opened its mouth and bit the tip of my finger. Quickly, I pulled my hand back and I inspected the tip of my finger but fortunately it had not injured me. The creature remained still, watching my every move. Nee'sa remained still, observing this strange creature's interaction with me. Again I moved my hand over to the creature, this time extending my fingers to gently pet it under its ear. The creature responded by coming closer and nuzzling my hand.

I have a new friend, I thought, as I continued petting its head. I gestured to Nee'sa to see if she could pet it as well. Soon it was making strange clucking and purring sounds as she scratched behind its ears and the top of its head.

Suddenly the creature stood up and froze, staring through the undergrowth. The fur on its back stood on end. Then I heard it, the heavy tramping of men's footsteps moving along a pathway. I could not hear any voices so was unable to ascertain whether friend or foe. We would have seemed an odd trio, as still as the night and staring through the shrubbery at the source of the noise.

We waited until the noise had long passed, and then waited some more. I slowly arose from my hiding place and crept towards the path, our little furry friend bouncing after me with Nee'sa tiptoeing close behind. Remaining aware of our surroundings, we silently made our way through the scrub until we came to a well-used path through the trees. Checking each way and ensuring that we were safe, we trudged along the worn dirt trail. Rounding a bend, we noticed a clearing ahead which would probably mean a village and the possibility of food and hospitality. As we closed nearer, we found a large area surrounding a low hill covered in grasses of all kinds gently swaying in the slight breeze. At the crest of the rise was a small village of maybe 15 to 20 dwellings, much the same type of construction we had already seen. What struck me as particularly interesting was that, unlike all the previous villages, this one had no defensive wall surrounding it. I took this as a good sign.

Holding each other's hand, possibly for moral support or maybe just for the pleasure of each other's company, we boldly strolled up the path into the village. No-one challenged us and a few people working in the fields nodded their heads in acknowledgement, curiously staring at our strange threesome.

With our eyes consciously watching around us, we entered the village. A collection of residents congregated ahead of us as we cautiously approached them. The group parted and a grizzled and bent old woman limped between them to stop directly in front of us.

Gesturing to Nee'sa to remain quiet, I spoke in the language of the Siculi.

"We mean no harm to your village. We come alone."

The old woman looked directly into my face, then passed a sideways glance at Nee'sa. She then suddenly bent her head to fix her eyes on the knife sheathed in my belt, slowly lowering her head further to stare at our furry companion. She leaned forward so that her gnarled fingers gripped the handle of the knife and she slowly slipped it from my belt to drop it on the ground. Our furry friend jumped out of the way and scurried away well out of sight.

Fearful from experience and to try and give an impression of harmlessness, I raised my hands high.

"Hsst!! Put your hands down, you little fool. We are not here to hurt." The old woman said

I looked at her puzzled.

"You look hungry, my pilgrims," she continued in a softer voice, "come. We will feed you."

She beckoned to several of the villagers to follow and we were led off to a large hut near the centre of the village. We passed through a heavy leather curtain into the hut. The pungent smell of damp earth and wood smoke rocked our senses as our eyes adjusted to the gloom. Soon, we could make out a newly lit fire crackling in the hearth in the centre of the hut and the mounds of skins and cloth of sleeping places.

"Sit!" The old woman commanded. We noted that there were thickly padded cushions next to us which we gratefully sat upon. The curtain at the entrance parted filling the interior of the hut in bright sunlight. Several young women ducked through the doorway carrying dishes of steaming food which they set down in front of us. Another slightly older woman placed a bowl of freshly baked bread amongst the other dishes. It was only then that I noticed the old woman was sitting opposite us on a rickety frame.

"Eat!" She commanded. We gorged ourselves on the first meal we had eaten in quite a few days. As we stuffed ourselves, the old woman looked at us closely, observing us and reading us.

"You are from the island!" She stated abruptly as we paused in our eating.

"Huh?" I grunted questioningly with a mouth barely empty.

"The island!" She stated again, "you speak the language of the Siculi. But you do not dress like them, but from somewhere more distant."

I looked into her hollow dark eyes. I could neither see nor sense anything.

"We are from an island near the Siculi," I began to explain. "We lived with the Seculi for a while before being brought here – wherever here is. I know it is far from the Siculi and an even longer way from our home."

"Ah!" She nodded in understanding, "you are from Melita. You are the one the Ancients spoke about." She stressed the 'are' as if she had known about me for a long time.

Then, in Meliti she said, "the ones of old have told us that a young man from the island will come here on his journey to write his people's story. I believe that man is you. We have waited a long time for you to come."

Then staring at Nee'sa, she said slowly, "the ancients spoke not of any companions. However, I can understand the company of you, girl, but your missing hairy friend I cannot! But, nonetheless, you are here, my dear. Our hospitality extends to all."

Rising with effort, the old woman ceremoniously flicked her robe behind her and glared at me again.

"My name is Zagara and we will talk again on the morrow, young Ka'desh." Her voice vanished out the doorway along with her presence.

Nee'sa turned to me puzzled.

"She knew your name. How would she know that unless she is a very powerful sorcerer?" She mused. Then with a twinkle in her eye she continued, "there is more to you, my Deshi, than I thought. You are a mysterious one."

Fully sated now from the food offerings we were given, we lay down on the skins and very quickly fell asleep in each other's arms. The feeling of Nee'sa's soft skin against mine was intoxicating and was probably an influence on my dreams that night. I knew without doubt that I had found my life partner again and that the ancients were wrong.

We awoke to two young women bringing us freshly baked bread with berries and nuts for our morning meal. They tittered and giggled at us as we devoured the food. Nee'sa's curiosity got the better of her and she reproached the girls.

"What are you twittering about, you two? It is as if you have been caught holding hands with a young warrior of your village for the first time."

"We are very sorry, mistress," one spoke, "but we have never met anyone whom our ancients told of before in our folklore. We always thought that the stories were the stories that old men told around the evening fire."

"So why are you still here?" I demanded, seeking a little privacy.

"Oh master," the other blushed, "we have been instructed by Zagara to wait on you and tend to your every need. You are the talk of the village and Josti and I are privileged to serve you."

"I am sorry," I said abruptly, "but we do not require your services."

Josti burst into tears.

"Master, it is our duty to you. If we cannot do it, then we will have failed in that duty." She blubbered, "Vella and I must do it else Zagara will be displeased and the village will banish us."

"Just who is Zagara and what power does she hold?" Nee'sa demanded.

"She is our healer and spiritual leader. She is the chosen one who talks with our ancestors and the ancients. She may be old and frail, but there is nothing which she does not know. We have been apprenticed to her so must do her bidding." Vella explained.

Nee'sa and I exchanged glances.

"And how far does the bidding go?" I cheekily asked as I smirked in Nee'sa' direction. She responded with a sharp elbow to my ribs. I quietly groaned as the pain subsided and mouthed to her, what did you do that for? Her response was a sultry and cold stare in my direction, and a wave of dismissal to the two girls.

As they departed, Nee'sa glared at me with a look of disapproval.

"Don't do that again." She scowled at me.

"I think that you are jealous." I retorted, knowing full well that she was and that she would never admit it. It was at this point our furry little companion furtively re-emerged through the doorway and I realised that we hadn't name it. Well, we couldn't always refer to it as a "furry it" after all.

Nee'sa must have read my mind as she noticed it in the doorway.

"We should call it something," she observed, "what about Kura. That's a cute name for a cute creature."

"Well Kura it is then," I replied, and then looking straight at the now puzzled animal, continued, "Kura, you must come and join us."

Kura scampered across the dirt floor of the hut raising a small cloud of dust, finally jumping into the sleeping furs and snuggling in.

"Well, he is comfortable," Nee'sa laughed.

The doorway darkened and the familiar bent form of Zagara became apparent. She shuffled across to us and sat on her chair in the gloom. She waved her hand gesturing for us to sit. Kura poked his head up to observe from the relative safety of the furs.

Zagara glared at me.

"Do you know why you are here?" she demanded.

"No. Not really," I replied, "this prophecy thing keeps coming up but I am not sure that it is actually real. So far our journey has made little sense. We just seem to go from place to place with no real sense of purpose."

Zagara's glare became more intense.

"Everything you do, my young Ka'desh, has been preordained. Every step of your journey has been anticipated by the prophets of old. I can tell you every part of your journey thus far, because it has been told to me as well. Where you go to from here has already been written, but it is not for us yet to read. I do know that your journey is far from over, it will be long and heart-breaking and will endure for many a lifetime."

This made absolutely no sense to me and the quizzical looks which Nee'sa was giving me told me that she could not make any sense of it either.

We sat there dumbfounded as Zagara continued, She related my journey to the Siculi, the storm, our capture in the village and subsequent escape, and everything in between up to our present situation.

"What about the dreams you have had?" Nee'sa asked. It had been so long since I had last had one of those strange dreams, I had forgotten about them. Before I could say anything, Zagara interjected.

"You have had dreams, Ka'desh?" She asked earnestly, "can you explain them to me?"

I recounted as best as I could a few of the dreams and Zagara listened intently. Occasionally Nee'sa added what I may have omitted but Zagara's attention was solely on me. When I had finished, she just stared at me in silence for what seemed an age. Then she began to speak.

"Your dreams are your destiny; these visions are your future. That future may not be what will occur in the immediate time ahead but may be that which lays ahead many, many years."

She continued to explain as best she could most of the dreams as predictions of my journey thus far, however she was at a loss for a few of them, particularly the one where I looked down on my own body. She seemed to think that I was possibly in the company of the gods, but that anything else was beyond her comprehension.

After what seemed hours of talking, Zagara rose to go. She now had what seemed a twinkle in her eyes.

"I see you have no need for my apprentices then, Ka'desh," and with a smile she disappeared through the doorway.

"What did she mean by that, Deshi?" Nee'sa retorted.

I turned away from her with a smug smile on my face.

We spent several days in the village, mingling with the inhabitants who all seemed very welcoming. Kura kept his distance from any other humans, preferring to remain hidden in the bedding and only emerging when we had food to give him. I noted that the younger menfolk tended to avoid us, averting their gaze and whispering amongst themselves once we had passed. At first we were bemused, but after two days it was becoming annoying. One day after we had passed and the whispering began, I turned and confronted a group of four of them.

"What is it that you cannot say to our faces?" I demanded of them. Looking very sheepish at the sudden confrontation, they began to walk away, embarrassed. One, the tallest, turned on his heel and strode up to me.

"What makes you so special? You come to our village with your head filled with dreams and special attention. We have lived here all our lives and have had to earn any special attention. What do you want here?" He remonstrated to me.

"I am not, I mean we are not what you think." I reluctantly countered, "any special attention you perceive us getting is only because of old stories, very old stories. Your elders think that those stories are about me. They are not. I am not special. We are not special. We are just travellers from a distant land trying to find our future."

I felt I was beating my head against a temple wall and was losing the argument. The youths walked away silently. I began feeling that we needed to leave this village sooner rather than later. That evening I discussed this with Nee'sa, we decided that we would leave the following day, but we would speak to Zagara first. We could not fault the hospitality and friendliness of the village, however there were uncomfortable elements within that we could not ignore.

Early the following morning after our meal, Zagara listened to our concerns and was very understanding. She instructed Vella and Josti to gather some food and bundle it for us to take with us. Along with the food, we were also given a goatskin water canteen. As we began to say our heartfelt thanks and goodbyes, Vella and Josti both wrapped their arms around the two of us and squeezed us tightly.

"Goodbye and good fortune," they echoed in unison. Kura stood just behind, looking up at us all in bemusement. As we disentangled ourselves, Zagara spoke.

"May the fortunes of the gods and of all our ancestors be upon you. Your journey is still to be completed and there may be danger at every turn. Pray to your gods at every opportunity for their protection and guidance. I know we shamans will do the same."

Then pointing to the path, she continued, "follow the path for three days until you meet Vesuvo – you will know him by his fiery breath and scorched land. Any villages you may encounter should greet you warmly, as there are many pilgrims on this path. When you see Vesuvo, take the next path towards the sea. It is the only way you can avoid his dangerous breath. There is a large village on the seaside that they call Napoli. You would be safe there."

Then we were left alone, gazing up the well-trodden path meandering through the crops and into the trees ahead. We began our trek, three hapless pilgrims strolling as carefree as we could along the path. We must have seemed quite comical, Nee'sa and I sauntering side by side with our little furry friend, Kura, bouncing along behind us.

Each day, we walked along the path as instructed. Each day we would pass through several villages, each as welcoming as the last and each night accepted as guests to dine and sleep in comfort. Each morning, we would leave the warm hospitality to a banter of well wishes, our victuals replenished, to continue along the path. Our travels took us through light bushland and undulating fields of maize and corn, gently dancing in the slight breeze like the ebb and flow of the surface of a large pond. The beauty of the landscape did not escape us as we journeyed. We were in a dream which neither of us wanted to end. It was on the third day when it seemed that the dream had ended.

In the distance, we spotted a plume of dark grey and white cloud lazily wafting into the sky to spread across the horizon. I had a recollection of a similar sight in my past and I wracked my brain trying to remember when it dawned on me, I had seen a cloud such as this when I was with the Seculi. It had been Mongibello. A flash of red momentarily appeared amongst the plume followed by flashes of white. We stared at the mountain emerging in the distance and realised that its slopes were devoid of any vegetation. This, we realised, must be Vesuvo.

We followed the trail through a copse of trees, temporarily shielding Vesuvo from our sight. We could feel the earth pulsating under our feet in small tremors. Nee'sa stole a concerned look at me as Kura painfully climbed my leg to shiver in fright around my neck.

"Xi'tan," I mouthed back, absurdly thinking that he would not hear me.

We broke through the cover of the trees to a landscape drastically changed from the cool and temperate forest we had just been through, to a rocky, colourless and bleak vista of desolation. Trunks of trees poked their burnt remains up through the rocks, which appeared to have flowed like a river around them. Sharp extrusions pushed over the rolls of undulating black rock which, in stark contrast, streaked the sterile grey soil remaining.

We could discern the worn trail meandering around the boulders and rocky terrain, so followed it. As we strolled along, wisps of grey dust floated upwards to settle back to earth behind us to partially obscure our footprints. As the light from Sem'a began to dim, we saw another path branching to the left, down a steep slope. In the distance, we detected a thin blue line of water on the horizon and the tell-tale columns of smoke rising from what must be a substantial village. After some time passed, we dragged our weary bodies over yet another crest to see ahead of us an abrupt line between the bleak and lifeless greyness we had thus far struggled through, and the inviting greenery of trees and beyond, a field of corn wavering in a slight breeze. At the far edge of the corn field was a village so much larger than any we had yet seen.

"Napoli!" I exclaimed in awe, recalling what Zagara had instructed us some days ago. Nee'sa looked across at me smiling. If good fortune followed us tonight, we would have a good meal to fill our gut and a warm bed to sleep in. With much less caution than we would have previously exercised and feeling empowered by Zagara's counsel, we marched into the village.

The main path in the village seemed to weave its way around huts seemingly erected haphazardly and without purpose or planning. After several false paths and dead ends, we reached the village centre. People silently emerged from their huts to congregate inquisitively around us. Not a sound was heard except the scuffing of shoes on the hard earth. As the crowd thronged around us, hands began poking at Kura, who clung shivering to my neck, whilst others picked at our clothing, our hair and our scant belongings. Nee'sa began to panic as the crowd pushed closer to us. Voices began to be heard, first a low babble, then rising to a crescendo.

Suddenly a loud ululation was heard penetrating the noise of the crowd. The crowd silenced and then parted, allowing through a tall and gangly figure who was hideously painted in the dark grey powder from the slopes of Vesuvo. The only clothing the figure wore was a loin cloth covering its sexuality, making it difficult to see whether it was a male or female.

The figure pointed at us and gestured with its bony finger for us to follow. We pushed our way through the mob and the murmuring recommenced as we followed the figure to a large hut surrounded by jet black pillars of rock. Above the door, a huge ox skull with the horns still attached stretched across the lintel of the doorway. A confusingly noxious odour of burnt dung mixed with that of fragrant flowers wafted out of the doorway as we passed through.

Once inside, it was indicated that we stop and wait. The wraith-like figure disappeared into the gloom, soon to reappear wearing a long leather robe. As I stared at the figure in the gloom, I was truly reminded of the figures of Iskef and Veritani.

"I have been expecting you," the figure spoke to us in a shrill voice. It smiled at our surprise at its ability to speak the language of the Siculi.

"I am the village High priest and I am called Seculani," they continued in their falsetto voice. "The legends tell me that your name is Ka'desh. But I am not certain who your colleague and your little friend are."

I found my voice.

"This is my companion, Nee'sa and our furry friend is Kura. How did you know that we were coming?"

"Ah! The trees in the forests have ears and the wind carries everyone's secrets. The winds informed me that a seer named Zagara had sent you to us."

Nee'sa was a little less diplomatic than I.

"Are you man or woman?" She enquired.

"My dear, I am neither, yet I am both. I am man on the outside but in here," as they pointed to their chest, "I am woman. The gods chose me to be born this this way so that I could have no bias over gender or form. But enough now. I want to hear about your adventures. The winds, leaves and birds have spoken to me but," Seculani paused and winked to us, "sometimes they hear wrong."

It took several hours for both of us to recount our adventures – dwelling not on our trials and tribulations, no matter how painful. Seculani listened intently, occasionally interjecting for clarification, but on the whole nodding in interest. Twice through our discussion, food was discreetly brought in and the bowls deposited at our feet. A large pitcher of water stood beside our host, from which Seculani frequently dipped our drinking mugs into to sate our thirst.

When we had finished, Seculani stared at us with those black eyes, a low guttural moan emanating from deep within their body.

"It is interesting," they drawled in a lower tone, "the ancients were correct. It is you, young Ka'desh, that the legends speak of. The legends also spoke of you being a seer, one who sees the future. The dreams you tell me you have had confirm this but of their meaning I am unable to advise you. Have you had any in recent days?"

"No." I replied, "I think we have only been concerned with our own survival. We had been through some grievous times in the past and the experiences have not been lost on us."

I looked across to Nee'sa who nodded in agreement, then continued, "we are extremely grateful for your hospitality and that of the other villages we have visited in these last days."

"You are welcome to stay as our guests for as long as you think necessary." Seculani said as they rose. "You may stay in one of the smaller huts which the village has prepared for you in anticipation of your arrival. I think that you will find it comfortable and to your satisfaction. Come! Follow me."

We rose and followed Seculani out the doorway of their hut and past the black pillars. Kura had again climbed to the relative safety of my neck. It was only a short distance to our lodgings, which was a hut much smaller than most of the others in the village. On closer inspection, I saw that the walls were made from the black rock we had seen on the slopes of Vesuvo, bound together with a dark clay. The roofs were a thick thatch of branches and vines tightly interwoven. Inside was a small fireplace, hot coals simmering wisps of smoke up into the hole in the centre of the roof. To one side was a low table with eating utensils neatly stacked, and on the other side were two beds of sumptuous furs.

As weary as we were though, we were unable to rest. Instead, we left the confines of the hut and walked around the village. Kura had earlier left the sanctuary of my neck and had disappeared under the furs to curl up to sleep. As haphazard as the layout of the village first seemed, we came to realise that there was a simple reason for it. The village covered a large area, spread over the relative flat of a small headland overlooking the ocean. The huts at the outer edges of the village were crammed closely together, the paths between meandering apparently meaninglessly. It was then I thought of some of the more unfriendly villages we had encountered and realised that this was a defensive measure designed to hinder any rapid encroachment of an invader. As one made their way towards the centre of the village, the density of the huts decreased markedly to allow large open spaces between them, until the centre was reached where a low defensive wall, which we had neglected to see earlier, surrounded Seculani's hut. It was to me a discreet defensive arrangement without being conspicuous.

As Nee'sa and I sat on a large boulder overlooking the bay, we could not be anything but entranced by the waters glowing a brilliant blue in the afternoon sunshine. The water was so clear that one could plainly see fish swimming over the rocks and the sand at the bottom. We were spellbound and captivated by the similarities between this vista and the island we had left behind, what seemed now a lifetime ago. As Sem'a slowly slipped past the rim of our world and cast an eerie twilight, Nee'sa and I slowly made our way back into the village towards our new lodgings. Several villagers were still out and as we passed them, they smiled and bowed their heads at us. Bemused, we soon found our hut and were pleasantly surprised to find a large quantity of prepared food awaiting our arrival. After our walk, we were now ravenous and so gorged ourselves on the feast before us.

When we awoke the following morning, Sem'a was high in the sky. Bowls of fresh fruit and bread and a pitcher of fresh water had been placed inside the doorway to the hut. We arose and sleepily rubbed the night from our eyes and then washed our faces in the water from the pitcher. I moved the bowls of food to the table and we sat down, picking at the fare provided.

"What should we do this day?" I asked between mouthfuls of food.

Nee'sa cuffed me.

"Don't talk with food still in your mouth," she chastised as I hastily swallowed the food down, then continued, "I have a peculiar and unsettling feeling about this village. It is so much bigger that that we have encountered. I feel bad things will happen here."

I must admit that I had had a similar feeling but declined to show it. It was then I realised Kura was no longer with us.

"I know it is larger than other villages," I replied, "but they appear to be welcoming enough. Let us see how this day proceeds. Have you seen Kura? He does not seem to be with us."

I noticed that the skins Kura was sleeping in were disturbed and in complete disarray. It appeared as if someone had come into our hut while we were asleep and had taken him.

Seculani greeted us as we emerged from the hut. A large group of villagers stood behind.

"Where is your little friend?" Seculani asked. In their hand was a piece of blue coloured cloth.

Nee'sa and I looked at each other puzzled. The villagers did not look too pleased.

"We do not know." I responded, "he normally does not leave our side but he was not with us when we awoke."

We had tacitly agreed to not divulge what we had detected inside the hut.

"Then we appear to have a problem," Seculani continued, "the villagers inform me that one of the children was attacked by your creature. The child has been badly mauled and has breathed its last breath."

We were shocked at this revelation. He had been with us for quite a long time now and had never shown a vicious side. Seculani and the villagers wandered off to continue looking for the little miscreant. Nee'sa and I, too shocked to do anything else, wandered through the village to return to our boulder overlooking the bay. Passing one hut well apart from the others, we noticed a trail of reddish spots leading behind the hut. Following the trail, we came upon the remains of our little friend. His little body was torn apart and disembowelled, and as I turned his body over, I saw tufts of coarse black hair still held by his claws and in his mouth.

Suddenly there was a loud shout. Startled, we both turned to its source, and at the edge of the village a number of young men were struggling with the carcass of a large black bear. As they struggled closer, I saw the bear's face was stripped with long gashes across one eye and down to its jaw. Seculani and other villagers rushed up to the group of young men and crowded around them. Seculani stooped down to the bear's body and, prising its claw open, scooped out a scrap of blue cloth. At first puzzled, Seculani looked at the cloth fragment then over to us. I gently picked up Kura's broken carcass and carried it over to Seculani and displayed the tufts of black fur.

Seculani bowed to one knee and spoke quietly and carefully, "it appears that we have been mistaken. The courage of your animal friend has been revealed. A thousand pardons for our error. I hope that you may forgive us."

Nee'sa gripped my arm and we both looked at them into their dark eyes.

"I…we forgive you." I declared, "it seemed easy to arrive at the wrong answer. It is good that we know the truth."

Our little friend had not attacked the child at all but had sacrificed himself to try and protect it. A surge of pride rose in me but was quickly displaced by sadness. I had not recognized how emotionally attached I had become to our furry friend. I placed his body into a basket which was offered to me by one of the villagers.

I turned my attention to Nee'sa and saw that she was weeping. I took her hand and she fell into my embrace, sobbing on my neck. We were both going to miss that little creature.

In a small manner of recompense, and to acknowledge Kura's bravery, Seculani offered prayers over his body now wrapped in skins and tied securely. The bundle was then buried in a tiny hole within the High priest's hut, the dirt stamped down hard until it was almost like rock.

The body of the child was laid on an earthen mound at the edge of the village, surrounded and covered by garlands of local flowers. Her dainty arms were crossed across her chest with her favourite toy, a wooden figure of her father, clutched under her hands. The village menfolk then gathered mounds of dry timber and laid them about the mound until the girl's body could no longer be seen. Then at dusk, the villagers gathered about the mound. The girl's father held a lighted torch to the timber which quickly caught alight. Everyone chanted in unison an age-old ballad (I was told) over and over. The wretched parents were surrounded by close kin as they privately shared their grief. We remained around the fire until the last ember of the pyre died. It was early morning as we all slowly and sadly made our way back to our huts.

The next morning Nee'sa and I decided that we would leave Napoli. We called upon Seculani to bid our farewells, and after insisting that we not leave without adequate food and water, the High priest accompanied us some of the way along the path until the village was no longer visible.

"Farewell my travellers," Seculani bade us as we stopped and turned to each other, "may all the gods favours be bestowed upon you in the time ahead. Your story will be told, Ka'desh, and your ancestors will be honoured by your deeds."

As Nee'sa and I parted our ways with Seculani, we slowly strolled along the path, lost in our own thoughts and sorrow at the loss of a dear companion.

Soon the fields of grain made way to low shrubs and prickly gorse, which then became the drab dark grey and black of Vesuvo's cloak. We continued to walk in silence, only occasionally breaking the silence with the infrequent cry of pain when either of us stubbed a toe or scraped our arms against the sharp edges of the hard black rocks. The path meandered through low pillows of rock and down into deep gullies, all the time inching its way closer to the coast. We walked and staggered over the rough ground, not wanting to pause for rest until we had a more conducive place to stop. Bu'sa radiated her heat down on us as we struggled along the path. At one point the path ran under an overhang of rock, which gave us a little shade and temporary respite from the heat. We sat down on the rocks exhausted and took a small draught of water from the canteen skin we had been given. As we rested, we felt the ground shake beneath us, just a small tremor at first which quickly abated. A more severe tremor followed which gradually increased in intensity until we were afraid the rock above us would collapse. We hastily picked up our belongings and sprinted along the path until we were back in the open. The ground shook again, splintering rocks around us and cracking the path beneath our feet. We continued running, the ground shaking making it exceptionally difficult to remain upright and to continue straight. Fortunately, the path ran true and we persisted with our progress, however we did not realise that the path disappeared over a sharp crest to lead us right to a precipice.

The path narrowed and we soon appreciated the predicament we had placed ourselves in - the path ended at a ledge which wound down a cliff.

"We have done this before," I exclaimed to Nee'sa as she suddenly froze looking down the cliff.

Reassured, Nee'sa clung tightly to my hand behind me as I selected where to place my feet on the hazardous ledge, her grip reassuring me that everything would be fine. Luckily, the tremors ceased and our footholds became firmer. We slowly shuffled along the ledge, towards a leafy break in the rock ahead where the path appeared to go. Our hearts began beating at a slightly slower pace as we crept along. Bit by bit, the leafy sanctuary got closer.

Suddenly Nee'sa made a low noise followed by a blood curdling scream and I realised that I could no longer feel her hand. I turned around. My blood froze and my hair stood on end.

The path behind me had collapsed, the rocks crashing down the cliff face. I could see Nee'sa falling like a wet rag down the rock face, her scream now lost to the winds.

"Nee'sa!" I called frantically, hopefully. "Nee'sa!"

I watched her body bounce off the rocks below and stop like a discarded, bloody scrap on rocks, swept by the incoming waves. I started to tremble, distraught and overcome with emotion. Tears welled in my eyes as I squatted there in my grief on that narrow footpath, looking down at the shattered frame of the woman who could have been my life partner. I felt that I could no longer continue. I had an overwhelming urge to join her, to join her soul so that we could be together for all eternity. The gods prevailed as I realised that should I join her now, my soul would be forever tortured and would never be able to rest with those of our ancestors.

Recognising that I could not reach her, I stood up and composed myself as best I could, promising that once I was able, I needed to honour her in the best way that I could.

The evening shadows were beginning to cast their darkness about the cliff as I finally reached the glade in the cliff. I could still see Nee'sa's pitiful form floating back and forth in the sea, breaking on the rocks below. With tears stinging my eyes and my breath choking me as my chest tightened in pain, I rolled myself into a tight ball overcome with grief and eventually fell asleep. As reality overtook my heartache, I awoke from my dreams of that fateful moment. The remainder of the night I rested as much as I could in fits of sleep until the morning rays of Sem'a's smile awoke me.

Before I ate, I gathered as many rocks and pieces of wood I could find in the fissure and built a small cairn as a memorial to the love that I had lost.

Kneeling in front of the newly made memorial, I looked up into the heavens to my ancestors. Unable to voice a suitable epitaph, I could only visualise the events of the short time we had together. I then prostrated on the ground as a humble request to the gods to take the soul of Nee'sa to their abodes for eternity.

Briefly looking back down to the rocks below, I noticed that Nee'sa's broken body was gone, into Ba'hah's care until Bu'sa took her soul to her ancestors.

Heartbroken, I continued staring at the ocean washing over the rocks in a rush of foam below, then receding to begin the process again. Watching this made me weary and before long my head drooped and I fell asleep on the rocky ledge.

I dreamt that I was standing in the ruins of our temple at Ta'Shema. The walls had decayed and were laying at peculiar angles. The roof of the temple was long gone and where the village once lay, the remains of another, more strongly built temple stood. This temple must be the new one being constructed when I left. But it too was in ruins. The inside of this temple was blackened as if by a huge inferno. Each of the chambers of each temple was filled with earth, trees and grasses growing haphazardly amongst the fallen masonry. Nowhere nearby was there any evidence of habitation, although I could see tufts of smoke curling into the sky some distance away. I stood there puzzled, unable to comprehend the surroundings. Where had my people gone? What had happened? Where was my father, my mother, my brother, my cousins? There was no sign of any of them.

In panic, I wakened, all at once realising the potentially perilous situation that I had placed myself in on the narrow ledge. Regaining my composure, I carefully arose on my ledge, still puzzling over what I had seen in that dream.

Mountains

Unable to return the way Nee'sa and I had come due to the path's collapse, I gingerly clambered over rocks and onto miniscule ledges until I was standing on a pebbly beach. I took in my surroundings. Above and behind me the cliff towered menacingly. In front of me the sea crashed mercilessly against the shoaly shore. To my left was an impenetrable barrier of fallen and broken boulders, and my past. It was obvious then that my future lay to my right. As much as it aggrieved me to leave the place where my love remained, I knew that I should continue my quest, whatever that be and wherever it led. Carefully picking my way over the shoals, I slowly made my way along the shore, trying to remain clear of the crashing surf and stumbling over the loose pebbles and small stones which had washed up on the shore. After encountering a craggy headland, and with skinned limbs and painful joints, I agonisingly scaled it and descended to the other side, where I found myself looking along an extensive sandy beach with low dunes covered with spindly grasses rolling inland. Struggling to the top of the dunes, my legs sinking into the soft sand as I climbed, I breathlessly looked out and scanned my surroundings.

A short distance away the grass thinned out to low prickly shrubbery. Some 200 paces or so further was the beginnings of a forest. At one point there was a break in the trees, where I noted a worn path leading through the grass to the beach beyond. Exhausted, I eventually reached the path where I sat down to regain my energy. I still had a little water left in the skin and some nuts which had been given us at Napoli which I ravenously consumed.

As I arose, the weariness in my legs made them wobble, nearly collapsing beneath me. I fell to my knees and I squatted there for a few moments until I felt that my body was ready to continue. The path veered right around a large rotting tree trunk before continuing in a meandering route through the trees. At each turn, the forest was so thick that you could not see where you had been behind, nor where you intended to go ahead. The tree canopy above wrapped overhead blocking all but the fleeting flashes of light from Bu'sa's eye onto the path. In semi-darkness I stumbled along, unsure where I was headed and, to a certain degree, not caring.

Rounding the next corner in the path I lurched forward into a dazzling light, momentarily blinding me. The trees had parted and Bu'sa's glow shone down on me as my eyes became accustomed to the light. I found that I was standing at the edge of a field of corn, now long trampled by unknown feet. An ugly, thick pall of black smoke rose ominously over a crest in the distance. As I picked my way through the remains of the corn crop, I came across the long-deceased bodies of what appeared to be three youths. Due to their bodies decaying in the sun, I was unable to determine anything else except that the cause of their deaths was obvious, each of the youths had a number of arrows in their backs, and one had the shattered remains of a spear next to him. In shock at this scene, I gripped my stomach and my gut wretched violently before I sidestepped their mortal remains and continued towards the smoke.

Standing on the crest, I looked down at the remains of the village. Every structure had been ransacked, destroyed and burnt. The bodies of men and boys lay grotesquely where they were slain. Weapons of all sorts lay broken and scattered throughout what ruins remained. Curiously, I saw no trace of children or womenfolk at first, but this was to change very shortly. At one side of the village was the village well – a deep hole dug into the ground and surrounded by a low stone wall. I could see scavenger birds flocking around it, fighting and squawking. I made my way to the well and peered over the wall. Immediately my stomach heaved and I retched again onto the ground. Inside the wall lay the broken and dismembered bodies of children and old women. I fell to my knees and wept uncontrollably; I wept for the villagers' souls, I wept for the menfolk, women and children. And then anger overcame me as I reviled those who could callously perform such a deed. To me this action was incomprehensible. I realised that there were no older girls nor young women amongst the victims and this caused me to understand that the perpetrators of this horrific wrongdoing must have spared them, possibly as slaves or worse.

I wandered dumbfounded around the wreckage that once was a village. Devastation and murder were everywhere I looked. I was overwhelmed by the sheer stupidity and violence which had taken place here. I stood in the centre of the village with my head raised to the sky, to the gods, tears streaming down my face. As I recovered my composure, I thought that much as I desired to honour by internment each and every person slain there, there were too many to do so. All I could do was to leave, but not without a dedication to my gods for their souls. I formed a stone circle in the centre of the village and gathered what dry timber I could find to build a fire. Making a torch, I ignited it in the live coals of one of the destroyed huts. I held the torch to the timber I had prepared and as I watched the tongues of fire lick at the dry timber and climb upwards, I raised my head to the sky to see Sem'a looking down upon me through the wisps of grey smoke, disregarding any danger that the smoke may have brought.

"Oh great gods of this world," I sang, "please be kind and merciful. Take the souls of these unfortunates and lead them to their ancestors. I beseech you in the name of mine own."

I collapsed on the ground and remained there until the fire buckled into a shower of sparks.

After restocking with what water and food I could find which had not been spoiled, I warily departed the village. The path leading from the village showed obvious evidence of many people having recently used it, There were signs of some having walked, but there were other blatant signs of people struggling or being forcibly moved. The spore appeared several days old, but it did make me extra vigilant.

For several days I followed the path avoiding any villages and civilisation, the memory of the massacre at the village still very fresh. When my food stocks dwindled, I would resort to sneaking into a village at night and pilfering whatever I could, departing as quickly as possible to avoid discovery. At times, when the trees thinned sufficiently, I found that the path became obscure and hard to define, and it would take me some time to find it again. Once back on the well-trodden track, I continued my travels, not certain where I was headed and with even less certainty why. At times I could spot evidence of the raiding party – cold ashes of a fire, trampled brush and grass and the litter of hastily taken meals. When these were encountered, my senses became heightened and I would pass them warily, regardless of the fact that they had been long gone.

Water was seldom a problem, as there were ample streams and creeks from which to drink when I was thirsty. However, hunger was beginning to take its toll on me. There were many trees laden with berries but I was unsure whether these were safe to eat. A few wild olive trees loaded with juicy ripe olives presented themselves to me at one point, which I greedily consumed. This provided enough sustenance for me to survive yet a few more days.

The path meandered through groves and woods and up and down ever steeper inclines and higher hills. Up to this point the coast and sea were still visible at most times. After climbing one particularly steep hill, I looked down to see that the path travelled inland away from the coast. In the immediate distance I could define mountains crested by strange white canopies. As the days passed, the air became cooler and it became obvious that I would need some warmer clothing to ward off any chill. The clothing I was wearing was getting extremely worn and thin and incapable of keeping me comfortable. It was only the fear of encountering the wretches who desecrated that village so many days ago which drove me onwards, without thought for my own warmth and comfort.

It had now been several weeks since Nee'sa and I had departed Napoli. I had no idea where I was nor how far I had come. Each day was a trial of starting out a little after daylight and stopping when it became too dark to see clearly. My naked feet were now gnarled like leather from the incessant walking. My body ached and my stomach grumbled as I stumbled along each day, climbing higher and higher into the mountains. The forest had changed too, from the low woody shrubs near the coast, to the high twisted trees of the hinterland and now to tall, straight and lean trees with leaves like thick needles which towered above me. The night-times were different too. The animal sounds which up until now had not bothered me, were now distant guttural growls and roars which reverberated throughout the hills.

Early one evening after an extremely arduous day climbing ever higher up the steep slopes, I stumbled and fell onto a bed of tree needles laying on the ground. As I lay there, I imagined that I was on a soft cushion. My body was too weak, exhausted, tired and cold to resist or complain. I fell into a deep sleep from which I was sure I would never wake. For the first time in many months, I had another of my dreams.

A bright white light accosted my senses. There were figures dressed in white hovering over and around me. Above me was the sky, blue as the sky at my home in Ta'Shema, with strands of clouds scudding across. To one side were the branches of a tree in blossom with pretty blue flowers, but as serene as this vision appeared, there was something odd about the sky which I could see. The blue and the clouds were framed in strange boxes like a lattice of sticks and there was no movement there. It was then that I became aware of a low noise and I felt my body move, then it was devoured by a perfectly rounded yellow tunnel. The noise became louder, like a swarm of hornets congregating on a field of blossoms. It pulsated and hummed, penetrating my senses. The buzzing became louder, then became angry, growling at me in bursts of noise. I was frightened. The noises continued for what seemed to be an eternity before I re-emerged into the blinding light to see the figures around me again murmuring amongst themselves.

Then I was awakened. Something was pressing against my arm – something hard and sharp. Something else shoved my legs abruptly, and I weakly opened my eyes to the flood of a glaring light, momentarily blinding me. Suddenly I was drenched by a flood of water over my face, and I rolled over spluttering and choking amidst my incessant shivering. I looked up to see what appeared to be a savage beast towering over me, prodding my arm with an evil looking hunting axe. He glowered down at me through thick set eyes, peering through a wizened face of matted hair. The hair on his head was tied back behind his head by a leather thong and almost hidden by a furry bonnet adorning the top of his head. He was dressed in a long leather cloak, his legs were covered by matching leather leggings and he had a loose robe of woven grass about his shoulders. On his feet were a pair of wide leather coverings, the type of which I had never encountered before.

Loud raucous laughter greeted me as I looked around nervously at my accosters. Four more men stared down at me. They were all similarly dressed and heavily armed with deadly looking knives in their belts, a bow strung across their shoulders and a quiver full of arrows slung across their backs. They spoke to me in a dialect I could not understand. I spoke back to them in Siculi, hoping beyond hope that they might understand.

"Who are you?" I croaked.

"See," one said in passable Siculi, "He is not a savage after all. He speaks the same tongue as my cousins."

They all broke out laughing as they dragged me to my feet. All at once I feared for my life, thinking that these men were from the raiding party.

"Well, little one," the one who initially spoke continued, "where do you come from? You sound as if you are a long way from home!"

Something in his voice allayed my concerns and I relaxed somewhat.

"Then you can understand me," I replied hesitantly, "I have travelled for a long time and my journey has been too long to tell you here. My name is Ka'desh and I am from an island called Melita."

The men all looked at each other in astonishment then nodded knowingly.

"This is the one Bontag is looking for," one said to the others, "we must take this one to him. We cannot linger any more as it is far too dangerous here. Come. Follow us."

They turned and started though the trees. The one who initially spoke turned to me, took his cape from his shoulders and handed it to me. I graciously accepted it, wrapping it around my own shoulders and feeling its warmth envelop me.

"My name is Chabish," he said to me. I nodded in acknowledgement as our feet softly padded through the pine needle carpet. The cape across my shoulders was doing its job as my shivering had ceased, but my hunger had grown. I was ravenous and thirsty.

It seemed that we had been walking for hours. I stumbled along behind them trying my hardest to keep up. They walked with long loping strides, evidently well used to the terrain we followed. Although seemingly agile as they strode through the forest, I noted that Chabish had an unusual gait. He seemed to lope rather than walk, with a very slight limp on both legs. Striving to keep up, I found that my breathing was now much heavier and it seemed that it was becoming more difficult. Chabish noted my struggle, and calling the others to a halt, turned back to me.

"I am regretful at our haste and our forgetfulness that you are not of the mountains," he said to me in an almost paternal tone, "the air we breathe here is not the same as on the plains below. We need to take deeper mouthfuls so that we may breathe easier. We are also concerned that there are other tribes around who are not quite as welcoming as we are."

I related to him the devastation I had seen in the village I had been through. I had no reckoning as to how long ago it had happened, but the images were still very vivid and fresh in my mind. Chabish listened carefully, taking in my every word and pondering on them. Every now and then he would interrupt and question some aspect I related for clarification. Eventually I had finished and Chabish turned to his companions and spoke in their own tongue. Then he turned back to me.

"We will pause and eat. You will need your strength because we have a long way to go and we must travel quickly. It is urgent that Bontag be informed of what you have told me."

"Who is Bontag?" I asked inquisitively.

"He is the leader of our village," Chabish responded, "and he is a senior clansman of the tribes in our region. I am also an elder of our village, but my position is not as high as that of Bontag."

We quickly ate some dried meat, bread and nuts. After a healthy swag of water from a canteen one of the others had, I felt invigorated and ready for this new challenge. We set off again, the four men in front and me scarpering behind, just managing to stay with them.

We walked onwards until dusk when the shadows made it too difficult to see, when we had another light meal and then slept.

The morning light was just emerging when I was awoken. We silently and quickly packed our meagre belongings and set off once more. This day was very much the same as the previous, until late in the afternoon when we climbed a steep crest to halt and look down on a large village in the valley below. It was surrounded by meadows of long grass blowing over in the breeze as if water on a pond.

"This is our home," Chabish casually remarked to me as we walked down a well-trodden path which disappeared between the huts. A group of men were congregated in a large space in the centre of the village. One man dominated the others, not only with his air of authority but also his stature. He stood a good head height over his contemporaries, his body, though lean with age and experience, appeared strong and muscular. He wore a long cloak of leathered animal skin, artfully decorated with lines of purple and blue dye and embossed with outlines of strange and fierce (to me at least) animals. His eyes were black and penetrating as he stared at us approaching. His gaze fixed on me as our group approached him. Chabish had no need of introducing me – Bontag had already determined who I was. Whether this was by providence, from word of mouth or by legend, I had no idea.

Chabish engaged Bontag in a private conversation. On several occasions they looked directly at me, but otherwise the discussion remained private. When Chabish had finished his exchange, Bontag grunted and turned to face me.

"So, we finally come face to face, Ka'desh." He glowered at me. "I have known of your coming for a long time, in fact my forebears had spoken of your advent. Your name and your quest has been immortalised in legend and passed down from generation to generation. I and my village are honoured to receive you. Your quest is truly the subject of long-lost myths."

I opened my mouth to answer but initially only a croak emanated forth, much to the amusement of the gathering there. Finding my voice I said, "I am not worthy of your honour, O great one, but I feel privileged to accept it. What my task ahead is has yet to reveal itself to me, but from what has been impressed upon me, it has been preordained that I have an important role in my people's story."

"You will remain here for as long as you think necessary as our guest, as my guest." Bontag continued, "Chabish, I am certain, would be honoured to act as your guide, companion and confidante during your stay with us. Welcome to Bolzan, young Ka'desh. This is our village and our land."

I had the feeling that Chabish was slightly embarrassed at this sudden intrusion into his private life, but he did not outwardly show it. As his companions slowly drifted away to their own lives, he turned to me.

"I guess we are now companions, Ka'desh. Well, this night is now too late to establish any lodgings for you so you will have to be my guest in my family's home. My parents and my children will be honoured to meet the subject of an age-old legend. But before you meet my family, we must clean the grime of our travels."

At this invitation, I joined him at the well where we could draw water to attend to our ablutions. We were both very tired and dirty from our trek and needed to refresh our bodies, lest others be disgusted by our odours. As Chabish stripped his cloak and tunic from his body, I saw for the first time lines in his skin on his wrists and back. He noticed me staring at them and turned to me with a serious look.

"You wonder what the marks are." He commented, "They are the marks of a well-travelled body. At times the gods let me know that it is nearly my time to stop wandering this world and the lines are a sign to the gods to relent just a little and allow me to finish what I have started."

With a wink he covered himself again with his coat and cape and turned back to return to the hut.

"Haven't you finished yet?" He mischievously asked as he turned back to me smiling.

I hurriedly finished, dressed myself and joined him marching along the path towards a distant hut. It struck me that he had not mentioned his wife, only his children. I thought it would be a little intrusive at this stage to ask, so I remained quiet.

I remained as a guest of Chabish and his family for several days while an abandoned hut nearby was restored fit to use. It was during this time Chabish and I had many conversations about each other's lives. I learnt that Chabish had indeed been wed but his wife passed on to her ancestors during the difficult birth of their second child. The two children- a girl now almost of age to find her own partner in the world and a boy, a garrulous and lively young lad of only ten years - were the life and soul of their doting father. Each night the two of them sat at their father's feet, the flickering flames casting twinkles of light onto their innocent faces, as they listened intently to the stories of my travels. They adored their father and he them. I occasionally felt a twinge of sadness when I gazed at them and remembered my own childhood.

One morning, Chabish roused me with his foot as he was often wont to do. His reasoning for this, he once explained, was that when he was a very young and inexperienced whelp on a hunting party, on the first night when he went to awaken the next person to be on watch. However, instead of grabbing the person's shoulder to shake, he inadvertently grabbed the wrong appendage of the person asleep, much to the mirth of his companions and his own deep embarrassment.

"It appears that your hut has been complete and is ready for your residence," he beamed at me, as I rubbed my eyes squinting up at him. "We can inspect it if you wish after you have washed and eaten."

I arose and washed my face and upper body in a large bowl of water and ate of some coarse seeded bread, dried fruit and a drink of water. I ducked through the small doorway of the hut outside to find the air damp and the ground wet from recent rain. Chabish wore a grin from ear to ear as he beckoned me to follow. We stopped outside a hut somewhat smaller than Chabish's, but highly decorated with streaks of red, black and white diagonal slashes of ochre around the mud brick walls. When we went inside and our eyes had become accustomed to the gloom, piles of thick animal pelts crowded one side while an ornately carved stool and short table stood on the other side. In the centre was a rock hearth with glowing coals of a warm fire.

"This is too much!" I objected, "It is way too much. It is nothing I deserve!"

"It is what the villagers wanted to bestow on one so favoured by the gods," Chabish said as he shrugged his shoulders, "it is all yours."

As he stooped to leave me awestruck in the hut, he turned to me.

"And by the by, we start work again tomorrow." He smiled, "you are to be my apprentice."

Chabish disappeared from sight, chuckling away to himself as I retired to my new home.

That night I slept soundly, troubled only by yet another dream.

There were figures dancing in front of my eyes, black figures, all aligned neatly across a white background. At first they seemed meaningless, some looking as if they represented animals but as I looked closer the resemblance became less clear. More lines of figures appeared still on that white background, and as I scrutinised each one, they all became clear to me and that I could understand them. They magically formed words which I could speak, meanings I could understand and in a language which I recognised. It was a story, one as old as the ages.

It told of a boy whose destiny was to travel his lifetime across the vast lands in order to write his people's history.

I awoke in a sweat, momentarily disoriented by my new surroundings. As I gathered my thoughts and emotions, I realised that it was not real and only my mind yet again playing more tricks on me. I was, however, deeply affected by the understanding that the story in my dream was my story. I quickly fell back into a deep sleep, only arising when Sem'a shone her light into my hut and onto my face. After eating some food, I was tending to my personal ablutions when Chabish entered to hasten me to my new chores.

The new vocation now chosen for me would have been unheard of in an earlier life but now was a necessity for my new life. At the side of the village, in a cleared area far from the living quarters, a number of covered fireplaces had been constructed and large quantities of cut dried timber lay neatly stacked nearby. Each fireplace consisted of a hard brick dome with a short column at the centre, rising to flare slightly outwards at its top. At the base of the dome was a large opening inside which I could see a raging fire. Opposite the opening was a smaller hole with a leather bag held between two sticks. One of the villagers was opening and closing the sticks, which enlarged then compressed the bag. Chabish explained that this was to force air into the fire, making it much hotter to allow the copper to melt- the device was called a bellows. The noise it made as it was expanded and collapsed reminded me of a big ox snorting, so its name was well chosen. The heat when one was close was stifling, so much so that one's skin tingled and reddened if they stayed close for too long.

Chabish stood at an opening into the furnace and stooped down to shove more timber into the fire. A cloud of black smoke puffed out from the top and then dissipated as the bellows fanned the flames brighter. Two others lifted a large crucible with two wooden poles carefully onto the chimney. Chunks of reddish-brown material were then placed into the crucible and in no time they glowed like the coals below, before melting like ice into the crucible. Intrigued, I stepped closer to have a clearer view but was quickly stopped by Chabish.

"Look," he warned as he placed a thin straw of grass into the glowing liquid. It immediately burst into flame and was rapidly consumed. Grateful for his intervention, I stepped back. Chabish then began to tell me what was happening.

This was a metal called copper which came in lumps called ingots, which the village traded from passing merchants. It was then melted and recast into tools and particularly now – weapons. To form the tools and weapons, the ingots of copper were placed into the earthenware crucibles as I had just seen, and then melted over the furnace. Then, with the greatest of care lifting the crucible with the molten metal off the fire, the metal would be gently poured into moulds where it would it would cool and harden before being plunged into cold water. Once cold, it could be pounded into its more useful shape with stone mallets. Short daggers were finished by riveting a wooden handle to its haft then slowly and carefully sharpening its edges. Arrow heads were fashioned in a similar fashion, although some hunters still preferred traditional bone arrowheads or even hardened willow tips.

Tools for digging the turf for crops were simpler affairs with no real finesse required after casting. They merely needed to be fitted to their handles and were then ready for use.

Daggers, arrow heads and spear heads were by far the most popular now with eager huntsmen preferring a more lethal method of protection. Although I had now grown well beyond my island upbringing, there was still a deep-seated revulsion within me to take a fellow human's life.

It was after many changes of the face of Ka'mah that my life had changed and I was now very much accepted as a villager. Although not as privileged as Chabish, being a village elder, it was through my friendship with him that I was privy to many of the day to day workings of the village. My life of forever moving on, forever wondering what would occur next, had come to an end. It seemed as though the "journey" I had undertaken, the prophecy I was meant to be fulfilling, was at its completion and it puzzled me. I approached Bontag to ask him of his views.

"I do not believe that your journey has ended, Ka'desh," Bontag mused to me. "The gods have said that you would re-write your people's history and that is yet to be completed. Your life will unravel it's mysteries as each day progresses. Be patient and all will be revealed in the fullness of time."

I came to the realisation that the gods must still have plans for me, but they were yet to reveal them.

Over the ensuing weeks and months, I was constantly with Chabish and his family. We became almost inseparable and much like kindred brothers. So much so that we now had pet names for each other, he calling me "Desh" or "Deshie" (which brought back memories for me of my mother), and I calling him "Bish". We would often be seen hunting together when there was little or no work at the furnaces, and we had developed a keen understanding of each other's talents and weaknesses when stalking animals. Our hunting forays often took us into the high country where the air was much thinner, cooler and more re-freshing. My body had long since acclimatised to the higher altitudes and so I had little difficulty coping now. Most of the time we stalked and hunted the wild deer found this high up, often returning with each of us staggering under the weight of a big buck's carcass on our backs. When the weather was wet and blustery, we would limit ourselves to the closer vicinity of the village, availing ourselves of the plentiful hare and occasionally that of a wild turkey or swan.

On one such foray, as we casually strolled along a well-used path that meandered through the crop fields towards the tree line ahead, Chabish and I were chatting about our lives and what may lie ahead.

"Do you think the gods will know our names when we die and go to meet our ancestors?" I pondered aloud.

"Well, they will certainly know yours!" Chabish laughingly answered, "it has been spoken enough among the ancients. As for me? I think that if they do not know my name, they will call me by the name of place where I die. Yes, that will be it."

I looked at him puzzled.

"Surely the gods know your name. You are an elder in the village. You are a successful hunter, and you are a devoted family man. The name Chabish will be heard in the whispers of the breeze in the trees for all eternity," I said earnestly.

Chabish shrugged his mighty shoulders and strode off.

"Maybe," he muttered, "maybe not. Only the winds of time shall know that."

We continued along the path, both lost in our thoughts of that moment. I did think that Chabish's response seemed rather strange. Turning our minds back to the task at hand, it was not long before we ended a relatively fruitful day's hunting by adding a wild goose and a young deer to our catch. Laden with our prey, we headed back to Bolzan.

Of course, we were not the only hunters in the village, although we would have liked to claim that we were the most prolific. It was to our dismay at times that the furnaces were to take a higher priority, but this still did not deter us from our

hunting, however soon a massive upheaval to our carefree lifestyle would be upon us.

Stories began circulating, originating from the hunting parties, that there were strange people fiercely armed coming down
from over the high country. There were also stories that other
villages had been laid waste by these gangs of armed warriors. It
had been noticed by our villagers that there were clouds of black
smoke beyond the distant hills, but many initially dismissed this
as new pasture being burnt in preparation for ploughing and
laying fallow.

One day a large group of strangers appeared at our village,
and when they spoke our tongue, we realised that they were of
our kin. Bontag conversed privately in his hut for several hours
with one who appeared to be their leader. When Bontag and the
stranger re-emerged, they strode to the centre of the village and
gathered everyone around them. He then gathered all the clan's
elders and the High priest, Isatru, to meet in the High priest's
hut. Chabish, being an elder, followed them in.

When they re-emerged looking very concerned, Chabish explained to us that there were definitely raiders from other parts
beyond the hills, and that they were extremely dangerous.

Bontag was warning us to use all caution if out hunting and
to place sentries around the village. I immediately recalled the
village I had encountered in my travels. Bish and I exchange
knowing looks.

"Yes, Desh," he said gravely, "it seems that they are the same
ones."

When a murmuring of anger and dissent arose- particularly
among the younger villagers- Bontag instantly put it down, ad-
vising that we were only farmers and that fighting would be
futile. We would defend ourselves if attacked, but we would not

run after them. He then advised that we remain armed at all times and that extreme care be taken when hunting.

Village life then returned to a semblance of normality, with the villagers continuing to tending their crops and animals. Chabish and I retreated to what we did best, tending the furnace to cast tools for the crops and more importantly now, weapons to protect our very livelihoods.

Several days later, Bish and I were out in the lower hills above the village looking for deer. We were both well-armed with bows and knives, and Bish also with a short spear. This was the time of year when Sem'a, was starting her long rest, so the days were colder and her breath now chilled the air. Thus far our hunt had been unfruitful as we had seen very little game and certainly none that we could get with either spear or arrow.

The area of our hunt was rocky and craggy with copses of thick fir trees in secluded valleys in the rocks. The first falls of snow had recently started and there were light fluffs of its coldness clinging precariously to the branches of the low shrubs and the thorns of the gorse bushes. We pulled our cloaks around our shoulders tighter to ward off the cold air as we pushed our way to another thicket of trees. Chabish grabbed my shoulder and we both froze on the spot. Gesturing ahead of us, Chabish pointed to a shadow lurking among the trees. As we peered into the gloom of the thicket, the shape slowly took the form of a fully grown buck deer, its antlers rattling against the tree trunks. We both sheathed arrows into our bows and parted to quietly stalk this new and unexpected prey. Silently, we gently pushed our way closer to the deer, bows at the ready. The buck had yet to hear our approach and oblivious to our presence, continued grazing among the trees. We both crouched and at the same time drew the loaded bowstrings back.

Suddenly we heard a scream; the deer shot its head up and listened. It then turned and melted back into the shadows of the forest.

Glacier

Suddenly they were all around us, shouting and swinging their weapons wildly. We turned, standing back to back, Chabish armed with his axe and flint knife, me with only a timber club. One of the savages lunged at me with his knife and I parried it easily with my club. He lunged again, this time with his other hand which carried a short spear. Searing pain shot up my side as the spear penetrated my tunic and lodged itself under my ribs. I staggered and fell to my knees. My head filled with the stars of night as a club came glancing off my skull as another savage entered the affray. I shook my head to clear it and as I arose, I picked up a discarded arrow from the ground. The savage came for me again, swinging his club high to crash it down on my skull. I leapt up, driving the arrow into the savage's mouth to the back of his throat. Blood bubbled from his mouth as he gurgled and slowly drowned in his own blood. I glanced quickly at Chabish and saw that he had despatched one savage and was in a fearsome tussle with another. I wrenched the arrow I had just used from the dead savage's mouth and, spinning around, managed to drive it under the ribcage of Chabish' assailant, penetrating his heart and instantly killing him. He fell limp, collapsing to the ground. I staggered to Chabish, holding the wound in my side. It was then that I saw that my friend was bleeding badly from a deep gash to his right hand. Although we were exhausted and badly wounded, we both knew what we must do next.

We ran as fast as we could to escape the remainder of the raiding party who were now gathering behind us. Upwards we ran, towards the snow and ice fields. Arrows whizzed past us, clattering amongst the stones. Chabish was running beside me, panting. Suddenly he grunted and stumbled, but quickly regained his step to resume running. The pain in my side was now crippling me and I was finding it extremely difficult to continue. I staggered and fell, my mind going hazy, then blank.

My head was swimming in a pool of darkness and I had a vague sensation of moving. Gradually, my head stopped spinning in the dark vortex and I slowly regained consciousness. Disoriented, I saw everything upside down. I then realised that I was being carried on Chabish' back as he scurried up the slope, dodging the arrows and spears being hurled our direction.

Reaching the summit of the ridge he collapsed, throwing me roughly onto the ground. I rolled painfully onto my back and looked across to my comrade laying on his face a short distance away. I dragged myself to my knees, and holding my hand over the agonising pain in my side, crawled to his still body. An arrow protruded obscenely from his left shoulder, blood oozing from around the wound. The back of his head was a mass of congealed blood knotting his hair and soaking his bearskin cap. Drawing myself up, I reached for the arrow and with all the strength I could summon, pulled it free from his shoulder. Blood spurted from the now open wound and Chabish moaned mournfully. My friend was dying; we were both dying. I cradled my friend in my arms

"Bish?" I asked, "can you get up?"

"Aargh!" He groaned as he looked up at me, coughing a spume of blood and saliva over his face. He could not speak. His eyes rolled back and he sighed. Then, with a gurgle, Chabish breathed his last and met his ancestors.

With tears welling in my eyes, I left my friend where he died as I crawled to the relative safety of a distant crest overlooking a sea of ice and snow. I could feel the soft sensation of fresh snow drops on my face as I dragged my tortured body over rocks and gravel. I looked up and could see the ample proportions of Bu'sa beckoning me to paradise. I crawled slowly, ever so slowly as I inched my way to the light. Momentarily my mind cleared, and I saw that it was Sem'a reflecting her light from the ice of the snow field. Disheartened, I stared at Sem'a's glow, trying to cry out in my suffering, pleading for Bu'sa to come and take me.

Soon darkness overcame me, and as I gripped the statuette hanging from my neck, I fell into the abyss of a deep, eternal sleep.

Fulfilment
(present day)

The television screen flickered to an image of a ridge of snow covered mountains, then panned to a group of people dressed in ski gear carrying a sealed composite plastic box. The box was almost coffin-like, long and thin, with the top closed shut by silver butterfly clips.

The camera switched its focus to a reporter, who turned his gaze from the group to the camera and raised a microphone.

"I am not far from the Italian border and I can feel an absolute buzz around me. Just days ago, the near perfectly preserved and mummified body of a prehistoric man was located by skiers just up on that ridge, buried in ice and snow. This spot is about four kilometres from the site where another mummified body was discovered in 1991. That body was called Otzi after the glacier near here where he was found. Amazingly, this discovery is remarkably like that of Otzi. There is speculation that both this and the body of Otzi are similarly dressed, and while there are few details available, the skiers who made the discovery say that it was clear that there are similarities between the two. Of particular interest is a small, carved figure found in the hand of this body. I overheard one person comment that it was curiously like the 5000-year-old "fat lady" figurines found in the temples of Malta. If that be true, then this is an extraordinary discovery. News has leaked out into the scientific world and palaeontologists, archaeologists and historians are all excitedly waiting to determine what further finds can be unearthed. I have been informed that this new information, in conjunction with that discovered with Otzi, could certainly rewrite the history books."

Author's Notes

My mother-in-law had a painting of the Grand Harbour of Malta hanging on the wall of her lounge room, and whenever I visited I would look upon that painting and wonder if it was really like that. That was about as far as my interest in the country went at the time. I had seen images in an encyclopaedia of the Maltese prehistoric sites but had never made any connection. My wife seldom spoke of Malta- her country of birth- because as immigrants to Australia in the early 1960's, she had deep feelings about the treatment she had received there in her younger years at school by many of her so-called peers.

Over the ensuing years social attitudes changed. Racism and discrimination diminished and thus, to my immense delight, her attitude to her heritage changed. In 2007 my wife travelled to Malta with her brother and his family to see their ailing father, from whom they had been estranged to a certain degree for over 30 years. When she returned, she showed me videos and photographs she had taken with her brother whilst there and my curiosity and interest piqued instantly.

Several visits later and having gained Maltese citizenship, I am now thoroughly ensconced in the island's history and its role and influence in the ancient and modern world. It was my approaching retirement that inspired me to pen a story, albeit a piece of fiction, about Malta.

At first it was challenging to find a theme on which to write but, by providence, I came upon an article concerning the discovery in 1991 of "Otzi the iceman", a well-preserved body of a prehistoric man found in a glacier in the Italian Alps. It was then that the genesis of an idea took root and I began to develop this story. Set five millennia ago, this is the fictionalised account of the life of Ka'desh, a young man from a village in Malta who, in order to fulfil a prophecy, travels far from his island home and ends his journey in the Italian Alps.

The natives of Malta from 3000BCE left no written records and their language has been long lost, so much of the colloquial language used in this story is based upon the modern Maltese language. Modern Maltese is a unique language with 10th century Arabic roots interspersed with mainly Latin, Italian, French and English influences. The name Melita is thought to be derived from the ancient Greek word for honey, the colour of the local limestone. Additionally, Melita was the name given to the island archipelago in Roman times as attested in the Acts of the Apostles in the Holy Bible.

The populated islands of the Maltese archipelago consist of the main island of Malta at just 27 kilometres long and 14 kilometres wide, Ghawdex (or Gozo) at just 14 kilometres by 7 kilometres, and Comino which is just 2.6 square kilometres in area. The islands have been inhabited since around 5900BCE. There are temple ruins at Tarxien, and the village temple where Ka'desh played is based on the ruin now called Tarxien Far East. This ruin is but a poor shadow of the- relatively speaking- more recent ruins preserved there. Likewise, there are well preserved ruins of temples at Ggantija on the island of Ghawdex, Hajar

Qim and the hypogeum of Hal Safflieni. All these sites are listed as historic sites by UNESCO, dating from between approximately 3600BCE and 2500BCE, and are under its protection. The island of Fifla lies just off the southern coast of Malta and appears to have been held with some regard by the prehistoric people of the island. Wied iz Zurrieq is a fishing village on the south of Malta adjacent to the Hajar Qim temples and is where boats depart to visit the famous Blue Grotto.

The "fat lady" of Malta is thought to represent a goddess of fertility, and has been found in many forms among the ruins of the Maltese temples. Although there is no face associated with the body, it is thought to be female and the figure has been found standing, sitting and reclining. Many of these artefacts can be found in the National Museum of Archaeology in Valletta, and copies in all its forms can be procured from most souvenir outlets on the islands.

Malta lies just 90 kilometres south of Sicily, and on a clear day Malta may be observed by the naked eye from the higher levels of Mount Etna, and indeed Mount Etna's eruptions can be clearly seen from Malta. As there is strong evidence of trade between Malta and the Sicilian islands from as far back as 5000BCE and probably earlier, sea passages between Malta and Sicily, and Sicily and the Italian mainland, would certainly have occurred during that time.

Up until now, a second "Iceman" has not been found.

Acknowledgements

Firstly, I would like to thank all the citizens of Malta for their fortitude and resilience over the past eight millennia. To overcome all they have endured has made their nation the one it is today.

Secondly, I need to thank all my co-workers at my previous employ, especially my managers and the girls at Ingleburn. Without their reassurance early on, this book may never have been completed.

Finally, I thank my family, particularly my wife who has always been at my side to offer words of encouragement when they have been needed most.

About the Author

Peter Shearing was born in Tasmania. Having spent his childhood growing up on a dairy farm in the north of the state, he joined the Australian Defense Forces while still in his teens and spent the following twenty seven years living around Australia with many deployments overseas.

On leaving the ADF, he and his wife moved back to Tasmania to enjoy a life of semi-retirement. This was short-lived as he decided to move back into the permanent workforce for another twenty years.

In 2021 he retired 'properly' and lives with his wife near Hobart, Tasmania so as to be close to family.

www.ingramcontent.com/pod-product-compliance
Lightning Source LLC
Chambersburg PA
CBHW020816190726
48285CB00006B/2306